Table of Contents

HUSBAND'S FANTASY BACKFIRES – BOOK 1

PETE ANDREWS

ABOUT THE AUTHOR

I write sexy romances. I used to publish under *xleglover* and *Flash of Stocking* on various sites.

My stories are romances, so they explore the feelings, emotions and relationships of the characters. My stories are also erotica, so the sex scenes are explicit. Often very explicit.

My stories have an emotional edge to them. The characters have thrilling adventures, but there's pain there too, at least for some of them.

I try to write stories that seem like real life. Yes, the situations are extreme, but I hope you come away thinking, *"Yes, I can see how that might happened."*

My wife is my muse, the love of my life. She is the Jennifer in my stories, the Sarahs, the Zoeys. Also also – *gulp* – the Jess's.

You can find my books wherever e-books are sold. If you'd like to join my mailing list or would like to send me a question or feedback, please email me at *peteandrews1701@gmail.com*.

CAST OF CHARACTERS

J*ess* – She's 38 with two young kids. She's been married to Rob for over 15 years. Jess is a 5'7" leggy blonde with small perky breasts. She's slim and in loose clothes, you might mistake her figure to be somewhat boyish. But no one looking at Jess would think she was anything but a girl. Not with her pretty face that lights up a room and looks like a glamorous model's when she does herself up.

Rob – He's 45 and fell in love with Jess the first moment he met her. He's partial to pretty blondes with long shapely legs, and that's all Jess. He knows he hit way about his batting average when he landed Jess, especially since he's older than her. Rob is average looking and, although he's a successful businessman, too many long hours sitting at the desk has made his body soft and out of shape.

Tina – She's 38 and has been BFF with Jess since high school. They were roommates all through college. Tina is somewhat short at 5'2". She's full-figured with a classic hourglass figure. Her legs aren't slim like Jess's, but they are shapely. Tina divorced Chris after she caught him cheating with a much younger girl. After a period of mourning over her failed marriage, she's gotten boy crazy – almost like she's punishing Chris – hooking up with one young man after another.

Darius – He's 25, white and tall, with thick wavy black hair that he usually wears slicked back off his face. He's Greek with a dark complexion. Darius is ruggedly handsome and has a bad boy swagger to him. Jess thinks of him as Mr. Tall-Dark-and-Handsome. This young man sports a serious package in his loose jeans. Jess and Tina have nicknamed Darius and his friends the *Stallions*.

CHAPTER 1

Jess walked into her bedroom, her face flushed from the conversation at lunch. Her pussy throbbed. She didn't normally masturbate in the middle of the day, but she needed relief, and the kids would be at the sitter's for a few more hours. She lay on the bed and pulled up her skirt. She touched herself. Her panties were so wet. She slipped her hand inside her panties and rubbed herself, her eyes closed, remembering what Tina had told her at lunch.

"Hey, what's this?" a surprised voice said from the doorway.

"Oh my god!" Jess cried in embarrassment, pulling the covers over her. "Rob, what are you doing home so early?"

Rob laughed, enjoying his wife's embarrassment. "My meeting ended early, so I decided to come home. I'm glad I did." Rob threw the covers off his wife. Her dress was still bunched around her waist, and he admired her long shapely legs. Even after 10 years of marriage, he couldn't get over how fantastic her legs were.

"Stop!" she protested, trying to pull the covers back up, but Rob laughed again and batted her hands away. Jess covered her blushing face with her hands. "I can't believe you caught me playing with myself."

"So, what got you so excited?" Rob asked as he put his hand on his wife's knee. Although, he thought he knew why his wife was so aroused in the middle of the day. "Did Tina tell you more about her sex life over lunch?"

"Oh my god, you won't believe what she did last night," Jess said excitedly. Tina and Jess had been best friends since high school and were roommates all through college. Tina divorced about six months ago, after catching her husband Chris cheating on her. Not yet ready for a serious relationship, but craving male companionship, she started going out with younger men about 2 months ago. Still pretty and desirable at 38, Tina pleasantly discovered that she didn't lack for male attention, and soon she was sleeping with a new young stud every few days.

"She met a guy at a bar last night," Jess said. "He was only 23, in grad school! She let him pick her up. He took her to his apartment, and his roommate was there. Both guys started flirting with her, and before she knew it all three were in bed! She ended up doing it with both of them!"

Rob took off his pants and boxers, and climbed between his wife's legs. "Did Tina like getting gangbanged by those two college kids?"

Jess moaned as her husband pushed into her. "She said it made her feel so slutty. She had one guy in her mouth, while the other was inside her. Then they traded places, and she felt so naughty tasting herself."

"Did they make her cum?" Rob grunted as he pumped his cock in and out of his wife's pussy.

"Yeah," Jess gasped, her own orgasm neared. "She said it was incredible. She'd cum with one guy, and then the other would take his place."

"Oh god!" Rob groaned as he came in his wife. Jess came too, her toes curling and digging into the mattress.

"Wow," Rob sighed a few minutes later. "That was great."

Jess giggled and poked her husband's side. "I bet you were thinking about Tina when you came," she teased. "You like hearing about how she's being so slutty. It turns you on. Come on, admit it. You think Tina's sexy. You can admit it, Robbie. I won't get mad."

"Okay, I admit it, Tina's attractive," Rob said honestly. "But you know what really turns me on? It's you, getting so excited hearing about Tina acting like a slut."

"What?" Jess asked, surprised.

"I'm not kidding. I guess in my head, I'm thinking you're wishing it was you, not Tina, going to bed with those young guys."

Jess's jaw dropped. "And that turns you on?" she asked feeling shocked. "Thinking about me with other men?"

Rob laughed. "Come on, don't be such a prude. There are a lot of guys with that fantasy. They even have a name for it, it's called the *'hot wife'* fantasy."

Jess glared at her husband. "I *know* what it's called, Larry, I don't live under a rock. I just never thought my husband was one of those perverts who wants to see his wife have sex with other men."

"Hey, wait a minute," Rob said, holding out his hands. "You're the one beating off in the middle of the day. Why are you getting mad at me?"

"I don't want to talk about it anymore," Jess said dismissively, getting out of bed and pulling down her dress. "Come on, the kids will be home soon."

CHAPTER 2

"What do you think of Jason, isn't he gorgeous?" Tina asked excitedly. Rob and Jess looked toward the restaurant door. Jason had gone outside for a smoke.

"Uh, yeah," Jess said. She felt awkward talking about Tina's new boy-toy in front of Rob. "Where did you meet him?"

Tina shrugged. "At a bar – where else?"

Rob laughed. "It must have been a college bar. What is he, 19?"

"Twenty-four, you jerk!" Tina said, playfully punching Rob in the arm. "And it wasn't a college bar, it was a hotel downtown."

"Excuse me," Jess said, standing up. "I have to go to the bathroom."

"I guess you don't approve of my new love life," Tina said to Rob as Jess walked away.

"That's not true. I know Chris treated you like shit, and you've had a rough year. A rough two years. I'm happy to see you're happy again."

Tina broke into a big smile. "Thanks for being so understanding." She reached under the table and squeezed Rob's thigh. "It's such a relief to hear you say that. I've been worried my friends would think less of me."

"No, not at all," Rob said, his voice caught in his voice. Tina's hand on his thigh made him shudder with excitement.

Tina was so different from Jess. Opposites. Tina was an attractive brunette with large breasts and womanly curves. Jess, in contrast, was a cute, leggy blonde with small perky breasts. Tina had a classic hourglass figure, while Jess was petite and, in loose clothes, one could mistake her figure to be somewhat boyish. No one seeing Jess would think she was anything but a girl, though. Not with her pretty face that could look like a glamorous model's if she did herself up.

TINA WASN'T LEGGY LIKE Jess – she was somewhat short at 5'2" whereas Jess was 5'5"—but her legs weren't bad – somewhat thick but shapely. Thinking about this, Rob's eyes wandered down to Tina's legs. Rob admired how, since her divorce, her skirts had gotten shorter and shorter. He also liked the way she wore fuck-me pumps with high stiletto heels.

Rob noticed that Tina's skirt had hiked up her legs. His eyes widened when he saw the lacy welt of her stockings. He realized she was wearing thigh highs! That surprised him; he didn't think girls wore them in real life. He thought things like that (real stockings and garter belts) were incredibly sexy, but Jess preferred pantyhose and only wore stockings on special occasions like their anniversary.

Tina followed Rob's eyes, and realized she was flashing her stocking tops. "Oops, sorry," she said, embarrassed. She pulled down her skirt. Tina shrugged. "Okay, I admit it, I'm a slut. But stockings are better than pantyhose – less fumbling and easier access."

"Uh, no problem," Rob sputtered, feeling uneasy. "Like I said, you're entitled."

Tina smiled, and again squeezed Rob's thigh. "Thanks, Robbie," she said gratefully. She let her hand linger on Rob's thigh. They looked into each other's eyes for a moment, an intimate moment between two friends. The moment was made even more intimate by Tina calling Rob, "*Robbie*," which was Jess's pet name for her husband.

Jess and Jason returned a few minutes later. As they ordered drinks and then studied the menu, Jason's hands were all over Tina. Tina giggled and pushed him away, but he was relentless, caressing her legs under the table. When the drinks arrived, he gulped down his beer, then stood up, pulling Tina up with him. "Come on, babe, let's get a smoke."

Giggling, Tina said "We'll be right back," then let Jason lead her outside.

Awkwardly, Rob and Jess continued to study their menus. Then Rob reached under the table to Jess's legs.

"Don't," Jess said giggling as Rob moved his hand under her skirt. But Rob wouldn't stop, and Jess gasped when he touched her pussy. She had soaked through her panties and pantyhose. Rob pulled his hand away when the waitress came to take their order. Rob told the waitress that their friends had gone out for a smoke. As he did, he smiled a wicked, mischievous smile at his wife. Jess hid behind her menu, not quite stifling a giggle.

"You're such a hound dog!" Jess playfully scolded when the waitress had left.

"You're the one who's soaking wet," Rob teased back.

About 10 minutes later, Tina and Jason finally returned. They ordered, and then Jason got up. "I need a smoke," he said.

Jess looked quizzically at Jason's disappearing form. "I thought you guys just had a smoke," she said. Jess looked at Tina, who had a mischievous smile on her face. "What?"

Tina hesitated, debating with herself whether she should tell them or keep quiet. But she couldn't hold it in. "Oh my god," she said elatedly. "Jason just did me!"

Jess's eyes grew wide. "You're kidding?"

"No!" Tina almost shouted, her face excited and covered with a big smile. "He pulled me into the alley next to the restaurant, and he did me against the wall! Oh my god, we were right around the corner, I could hear the people walking on the sidewalk!"

"Oh no," Tina said in a concerned voice.

"What's wrong?"

"I can feel him running out of me. I'll be right back, I have to go to the bathroom, I don't want the back of my dress to get wet."

When they got home from dinner, Rob paid the babysitter while Jess checked on the kids. Then, by silent agreement, they met at their bedroom. They groped each other like teenagers, practically ripping off each other's clothes.

"Fuck me!" Jess pleaded. Rob pulled off Jess's pantyhose and panties, then pulled out his hard cock.

"You so wet!" Rob growled as he penetrated his wife. "Did it turn you on, Jason fucking Tina in the alley like a whore?"

"Did it turn you on?" Jess answered as she pushed back against her husband's thrusts.

Rob's words came out between pants. "It turned me on, imagining it was *you* instead of Tina! Imagining Jason was fucking *you* against the wall!"

"Oh god, you're so bad," she moaned.

"I want to watch you act like Tina! Become a cougar! Let young guys pick you up, and go home with them and fuck them!"

"Oh god, Rob," Jess panted between moans. "You're so bad!"

"I want you to be my hot wife!" Rob said lustfully. "Didn't you see how muscular Jason was? Wouldn't you like to feel a young hard body on top of you? Ramming his big cock into you? Shooting gallons of his cum into you, so it floods out of you and runs down your legs?"

"God, that would be so slutty!" Jess cried as she raised her hips to meet her husband's thrusts. They were both so close, their passions fueled by their wicked fantasies.

"Yeah, yeah, and I know that's what you'd like, to act like a slut just like Tina, to be a fucking MILF! That's all I've been thinking about! You being a cougar and fucking all those young guys!"

"Oh god, oh god!" Jess cried as she came, Rob joining her just seconds after.

CHAPTER 3

"You haven't touched your lunch," Tina said after she finished telling Jess about her latest date with Jason.

"I'm sorry," Jess said. "I guess I'm distracted."

Tina reached over and grabbed her friend's hand. "What's wrong, honey? Are you and Rob okay?"

Jess looked up in surprise. "How did you know?"

"Jess, we've been friends since high school," Tina said, concern in her voice. "I was your maid of honor. I think I can tell when things aren't going right with you and your husband. So what's wrong?"

"It's just – god, this is so embarrassing. But I've told Rob some of the things you've told me. You know, about the dates you've had with younger guys. Lately, Rob's told me about some things he fantasizes about."

"Oh," Tina said, her interest suddenly more than just concern for her friend. Has Rob been fantasizing about sleeping with *her*? She remembered the dinner the other night, when she put her hand on his thigh. She shouldn't have teased him, but she couldn't resist. She could tell he was hard. It gave her a naughty thrill to flirt with her best friend's husband.

Jess hesitated, considering whether to tell Tina. But then she realized she needed to tell someone, and who better but her best friend? "You can't tell Rob I told you this," she said warily.

"I promise," Tina said immediately, trying to hide her intense curiosity.

"Rob told me that – he has fantasies about – about seeing me with other men."

"What?" Tina said, wide-eyed. "You and other men? Having sex with other men?"

"Yeah, I know, it's crazy. He's never mentioned it before. It's only been since you've been going out with younger guys. He even said he fantasized it was me who Jason did in the alley."

"Wow," Tina said, shocked. She had heard some men had this fantasy, but Rob seemed so conservative and strait-laced. Also, she remembered when Jess started dating Rob, over 15 years ago. Rob had been jealous of guys even speaking to Jess. Even looking at her. She couldn't believe Rob had changed so much, that now he'd like to watch Jess in bed with another man. "Do you think he really wants you to do it?"

"I'm not sure," Jess said looking uncertain. "I don't think so, but he always talks about it."

Tina considered her friend for a long moment. Then, impulsively, she blurted out, "Well, I think you should do it."

"What?" Jess said shocked. "Where did that come from?"

"Look, I'm not crazy. You won't believe how great sex is with these young men. They're so young and strong and gorgeous. And huge! And hard! I'm having the time of my life."

Jess looked doubtful. It wasn't too long ago that Tina couldn't stop crying after she found out Chris was cheating on her. And she had been a basket case during the weeks after her divorce was finalized. Tina might be having the time of her life, but it was just one meaningless hookup after another.

Tina didn't have anyone. She wasn't in a romantic relationship. She didn't have a man who loved her, and who she loved.

Tina shrugged, seeming to read her friend's thoughts. "Okay, I admit, my life isn't perfect. But *you* can have the best of both worlds! *You* can be married to a great guy who loves you, and fuck other guys on the side! Don't you see how lucky you are?"

Jess shook her head. "Having sex with other men isn't something I dreamed about when I got married. I mean, you're saying I should cheat on Rob."

"Jess, it's not cheating if Rob wants you to do it. If he knows about it," Tina insisted.

"I don't know about that," Jess said skeptically. "Besides, I don't know if Rob is really serious about this."

"What if he *is* serious? Would you play along?" Tina smiled affectionately at her friend. "I mean, it would be fun to have someone to go clubbing with, like we used to do in college."

"I don't know," Jess said looking uncertain. "Those days were a lot of fun. But I've been married for over 15 years, and I have two children. I love Rob. Okay, yes, he has these strange fantasies, and I admit, I'm kinda envious when you tell me your crazy stories, they're so exciting. But I love Rob, and I don't want to hurt our marriage."

"But Jess, honey, Rob *wants* you to do this. You won't be hurting anything. This might even improve your marriage."

Jess still looked doubtful. "I told you, I don't know if he really wants me to do this. God, I can't believe we're talking like this might actually happen!"

"Okay, I have an idea. Come clubbing with me Saturday night. Just you, not Rob. If he says no, then you know he's not serious."

"I don't know," Jess said warily, looking uncertain.

"Jess, what's the harm? This will help you and Rob figure out what he really wants. He probably doesn't know himself. And it's not like you have to let some guy pick you up. We can just go out and have fun, like we used to do in college."

Jess thought about it for a few moments, then she found herself nodding.

"CAN WE TALK?" JESS asked her husband. "I mean, we haven't really talked about the other night."

They were at dinner, at a downtown restaurant. Jess didn't want to talk about this in bed, or even at home. She wanted Rob to be thinking with his head and heart, not his penis.

"Sure," Rob said, putting down his menu. "It probably seems like my fantasy came out of nowhere, but it didn't. I've had these fantasies a long time, I just never had the courage to tell you."

"Really? Of watching me with other men?" Jess asked. She was shocked, but also intrigued.

"Yeah. It's always excited me, watching men flirt with you. Remember last year, at our vacation in Cancun, when that guy hit on you? He kept asking you to dance? I was so hard I thought I was going to burst through my pants."

Jess leaned back in her chair, feeling blown over by her husband's revelation. "Wow. Why didn't you tell me this before?"

"I don't know," Rob said, looking sheepish. "It's hard to tell your wife that you fantasize about other men fucking her. But I guess, well … lately, whenever Tina told you about one of her dates, you got really excited. And, well, we're done having kids. I've gotten the snip-snip." They both laughed at what they jokingly called Rob's vasectomy. His *snip-snip*.

Looking mischievous, Rob said, "I've been thinking maybe you might be open to some fun, before we get too settled down."

Jess frowned. "What kind of fun, Rob?"

"You know what I'm talking about," Rob said.

"No, Rob. I want you to say it. Tell me exactly what you want."

"Okay," Rob said. He was getting excited, and so he was trying to control his breathing. "I want you to go on dates with younger men. Men you're attracted to. Like Tina does."

"*Just* like Tina?" Jess asked. She wanted to find out how far Rob wanted her to go. "You know Tina lets them kiss her, right? You want me to let another man kiss me?"

"Yes, I do," Rob said without any hesitation. "As long as that's what you want."

"What about touching me? You want me to let another man feel my breasts? What if he reaches under my skirt? Should I let him do that, too?"

"Yes, god, I want you to let him do that!" Rob gasped excitely. "God, you've got me really turned on!"

Jess shook her head. "I don't understand how this turns you on. I mean, the thought of you with another woman ... it kills me just to think about it. But you get excited thinking of me with another man."

"I can't explain it, but it does. I mean, it makes me feel jealous, too. But, I don't know ... that makes it even more exciting." Rob looked around to make sure no one was looking. Then he took his wife's hand and lowered it to his crotch. "See?"

Jess's eyes grew wide with surprise. Rob was rock hard. His excitement was starting to turn *her* on. Also, she couldn't deny the allure of a young, hard body.

"Tina wants me to go out with her Saturday night," she announced.

Rob's eyes went wide with surprise. "She does?" he asked. "I think you should go!"

"Why?" Jess asked, acting coy. She massaged his erection. "Do you want me to do what we're talking about? Go have fun?"

"Oh god, yes!" Rob said excitedly. "I want you to flirt with other men! I want you to kiss them, and let them touch you! God, I want you to touch their cocks, and suck them, and even fuck them!"

Jess's breathing was heavy now. "Come on," she said urgently. "Let's pay the check, and go home!"

CHAPTER 4

Jess was going to be late. Tina was going to be there any minute, and Jess still wasn't dressed. It had been a long time (over 10 years!) since she had gone out dancing without Rob, and she didn't know what to wear. She finally picked out a silk, white blouse and a short black skirt. Underneath, she wore a bra, panties and black pantyhose. She finished the outfit with sensible, low-heeled black pumps.

Tina had already arrived when Jess finally came downstairs. She smiled when she saw her friend. "Wow, now I understand what husbands mean when they say it takes forever for their wives to get dressed," Tina teased.

"Sorry," Jess said sheepishly, kissing her friend on the cheek. "I couldn't figure out what to wear."

Tina eyed her friend. Jess had always been fashionable, and being a wife and mother hadn't changed that.

"God, you have great legs, I hate you," Tina said admiringly. Then, as if seeming to remember Rob was in the room, she added, "Don't you think so Rob?"

Rob could only nod; his throat was dry from excitement. Waiting downstairs for Jess to get dressed had been excruciating, but exciting too. All Rob could think about was his pretty wife in the arms of another man while dancing at the club. He was thrilled she had chosen to wear a mini-skirt, not pants.

Tina easily read the excitement on Rob's face. "Your pretty wife is sure going to be popular with the men at the club," she teased.

Rob tensed. How much had Jess told Tina about his fantasy? He had his answer when he caught his wife giving Tina the evil eye.

"I'll wait for you at the taxi," Tina said, a smile on her face. They had agreed on taxiing so they wouldn't have to worry about drinking and driving. As she left, she glanced at Rob, a twinkle in her eye.

Rob frowned. Jess shouldn't have told Tina about his fantasies, but then, they *were* best friends. He felt – what? Anger? Betrayal? Humiliation?

Rob's thoughts were interrupted by his wife's voice. "Well, I guess I better get going. Robbie, are you sure about this? You know, it's not too late to change our plans. All three of us could go out."

Rob looked at his beautiful wife. He found her almost impossible to resist, and he was tempted to take her to bed. But he knew her allure to other men would be just as great, even though she wasn't the tart and tease that Tina was. But then, some men – many men – might be attracted to Jessie's sweet innocence.

These thoughts and the prospect of Jess in another man's arms had gotten Rob so hard in his pants, it hurt. He was becoming obsessed by his fantasy of her with another man. The anger he had felt just a moment ago was replaced by intense lust.

"Yes, I'm sure," he said, his voice almost quivering from excitement. "Have fun with Tina and ... whoever. I'll be awake when you get home."

———◦———

"GOD, I CAN'T BELIEVE I'm here!" Jess said with disbelief written across her pretty face. She and Tina were sitting at the bar, sipping Cosmopolitans.

Tina smiled and squeezed Jess's arm. "Don't be nervous, we're gonna have fun. Don't worry about Rob. Who knows what happens to men as they get older? At least Rob isn't trying to sleep with other women. Like my shitty ex. I think you need to play this out, so Rob can get it out of his system."

"Yeah, I guess you're right," Jess said after a few moments. She still looked uncertain. "But ...."

"No buts, it's time to have fun!" Tina said laughing. She hopped off the bar stool and grabbed Jess's hand. "Come on, let's dance!"

Tina led Jess into the middle of the dance floor. It was crowded, so they danced close together. Jess felt inhibited at first, but soon started feeling more comfortable. She loved to dance, and began enjoying herself.

The music changed to a slow song, and Jess was about to go back to the bar when Tina grabbed her hand. She leaned close to Jess's ear and whispered, "Some cute guys are watching us. No, don't turn! Just follow my lead."

Tina moved close to Jess and danced slow. As she swayed, her fingers grazed across Jess's skirt. At times she pretended to whisper into Jess's ear, and as she did she allowed her fingers to trail down Jess's back. She edged even closer to Jess, until their breasts almost touched. Tina put her hands on her friend's waist, and they swayed to the soft music as one, Tina's fingers lightly caressing just above Jess's ass.

Jess inwardly smiled, knowing what Tina was doing. They had done this back in college, a little dirty dancing to get guys' attention. But that had been long ago – a lifetime ago—and Jess felt uncomfortable. She was married now, and had two kids! What was she doing here?

Still, Jess played along with her friend. She had to admit, acting so sexy and drawing so much male attention was exciting.

Jess was relieved when the song ended. Not waiting for Tina, she made her way back to the bar. She didn't want to give Tina a chance to dance another song. When Jess looked back, she saw Tina surrounded by guys. They all looked well under 25.

Most of the guys were in suits. Jess guessed they were attorneys just out of law school, or maybe Wall Street brokers. They were cute, but nothing special.

Jess was about to take a sip of her Cosmo when she saw him. He was tall, with thick wavy black hair, slicked back off his face. He had a dark complexion. Jess guessed he was Greek or Italian. He was ruggedly handsome, and had a bad boy swagger to him. He was Mr. *Tall-Dark-and-Handsome.*

He wore a black turtleneck, jeans and boots. Jess realized she was staring at him, and was about to turn away, when he turned towards her and locked eyes with her. His gaze was so intense it startled her, and she almost dropped her drink.

Embarrassed, Jess expected he would laugh at her, but he didn't. He just kept staring at her from across the room. After a few moments, Jess turned away, but it took a force of will to escape from his intense gaze. Feeling a little jittery, she finished the Cosmo and ordered another one.

A few minutes later Tina came back. "Come on, let's dance!" she shouted over the loud music of the DJ, dragging Jess off the stool.

"Wait," Jess said, and she quickly gulped down the newly delivered pink martini. Then she let Tina drag her back onto the dance floor.

The martinis were working their way through Jess's body, and helping her to lose her inhibitions. She was having fun, so when the music slowed, she didn't object when Tina moved closer for another round of dirty dancing.

"We got those guys so hot the last time!" Tina whispered gleefully into Jess's ear as they danced. "I thought they were going to drag me into a booth and rape me!"

As they danced, Tina reached lower so her fingertips trailed up Jess's legs. She didn't stop when she reached Jess's skirt, instead tracing up her thighs and bringing Jess's skirt up as she did so. Jess wondered if Tall-Dark-and-Handsome was watching her, and that thought combined with the two Cosmos made her more daring.

As they danced close, Jess lightly ran her fingers down Tina's back (she soon discovered her BFF wasn't wearing a bra, which didn't surprise her), then along Tina's curvy hips. Their faces were so close their lips were almost touching. As they slowly swayed back and forth, sometimes Jess's breasts would brush against Tina's. Whenever that happened, Jess felt Tina's boobs jiggle, since her tits were huge and she was braless.

The song ended, and as Jess and Tina stepped apart, the crowd applauded. Tina smiled and did a curtsy (flashing a little stocking top), but Jess was embarrassed and blushed. She quickly went back to the bar and ordered another Cosmo.

Jess looked around and saw that Tina had disappeared. Some of the guys were gone as well. Jess wondered if she would see Tina again that evening.

The new Cosmo arrived, and Jess was searching in her purse for her wallet when she heard a deep, husky voice behind her.

"I'll get that," the voice said, and Jess turned to see Tall-Dark-and-Handsome giving the bartender two 20s. Looking at the bartender, he added, "Keep it buddy."

Jess's heart did a back flip as she looked into his dark eyes. "Oh, that's not necessary," she stammered out.

"No problem. I'm Darius," he said, holding out his hand.

"Hi. Well, thanks for the drink," Jess said, taking his hand. Darius's hand was so large, Jess's hand disappeared within his. For some reason, it didn't surprise her that his hand was rough and calloused. "I'm, ah, I'm Jess. Darius – that's an unusual name."

"Yeah, it's Greek." *I was right,* Jess thought. *He's Greek.*

Darius made no move to release Jess's hand. Jess began feeling uncomfortable so she pulled her hand back.

"You dance really nice," Darius said.

Jess blushed again. "I guess it got a little bit out of control," she said feeling awkward. She was a mom! What was she doing in this meat market talking to this boy? She was probably 15 years older than him!

Darius smiled. "Well, you look good out there. You oughta lose control more often."

Jess laughed. "Thanks ... I guess." Then they both laughed.

"So, do you come here often?" Jess asked, but then she immediately put her head in her hands in embarrassment. "Oh god, I'm sorry. That's such a cliché." Why was she so nervous? She was acting like an idiot!

"No problem," Darius said, laughing. "Yeah, my friends and I come here every couple of weeks. It has a reputation for being a meat market, but we like the music. The DJ rocks."

Jess eyed Darius skeptically. That was like saying you liked *Playboy* for the articles.

"Soooooo, you're not here to pick up girls?" she asked.

Darius smiled mischievously. "That all depends on whether I meet a beautiful girl. Like you, for instance. I haven't been able to take my eyes off you all night."

"Not so fast, Mr. --."

Shit! She almost said Mr. Tall-Dark-And-Handsome! What was wrong with her?!

"—Mr. Cowboy," Jess sputtered.

Darius laughed. "Don't think I've ever been called *Mister* Cowboy," he joked. They both laughed.

Darius looked closely at Jess, and said, "I think you have the bluest eyes I've ever seen."

Jess laughed and shook her head. She couldn't believe how forward this young man was, but she guessed that's how it was nowadays.

She said, "First of all, I'm way older than you. What are you, 24?"

"Twenty-five," Darius corrected. "And you sure don't look older than me. I thought you were in college. Anyway, who cares about age? You're the best-looking girl I've seen in a long time."

"Well, I *am* older than you," Jess said. "I could've been your babysitter."

"That's super-hot!" Darius joked without missing a beat.

Jess laughed. She couldn't help feeling charmed by this young man. Also, she was glowing inside from his compliments.

"Yeah, well, anyways," she said with a dismissive wave of her hand. "Second, I'm a married girl." Jess held up her left hand, showing him her wedding ring. "See?"

Again without missing a beat, Darius waved his hand around the bar. "Most of the chicks here are married, but they're with other guys. That's how things are now. The next 9-11 could happen again tomorrow. We're all living on borrowed time. That's what people are doing now, living for the moment."

Jess eyed Darius. Then she frowned. Then she started to laugh. "Oh my god, that has got to be the worse pick-up line I've ever heard!"

Darius started to laugh too. "Hey, I worked hard to come up with that!"

"Well, I could tell you rehearsed it, but I think you should think of something else," Jess said, still laughing. "And it's horrible to use 9-11 to pick up girls."

Darius held up his hands in mock surrender. "Okay, okay, you win." Then he offered his hand to her. "So, do married girls dance?"

Jess considered for a moment. Tina was nowhere to be found. And Darius seemed nice enough. She took his hand, making a snap decision. "Sure, why not?" she said.

CHAPTER 5

Darius was a good dancer. His movements were slow and smooth, yet perfectly paced with the music. Jess couldn't believe a man as big as him could dance so well. He was well over 6 feet, and broad shouldered. She felt tiny next to him. As he moved to the music, Jess could see the muscles of his chest and arms rippling under his black turtleneck. His broad shoulders narrowed to a lean waist, and from what Jess could tell, Darius filled out his jeans really well.

Darius danced close to her, with barely any space between them. But he never touched her, never even brushed against her. Somehow, this close-almost-touching dancing, for song after song, was more of a turn on than if he was grinding his body against hers.

Eventually, the fast songs changed into a slow song. She expected Darius to pull her into an embrace, but he didn't. Instead, he stood there, so close to her but not touching her, looking at her with his intense black eyes, waiting for her to make a move. It was like he wanted Jess to surrender to him.

With a force of will, Jess stepped away. She said, "Ah, well, thanks for the dance. I guess I'll go try to find my friend."

Jess walked through the crowd looking for Tina, feeling a mix of disappointment and relief. And annoyance, too. Her nipples were hard, and she was soaking between her legs. For the first time since she started talking to Darius, she thought of Rob at home. He would probably be disappointed that Darius hadn't pulled her into his arms and danced a slow dance.

She was getting frustrated looking for Tina. Where was she? Jess walked into a secluded, darken part of the club, far away from the lights of the dance floor, when she felt a tap on her shoulder. She turned and there was Darius, standing just inches from her. "Oh, hi—."

Darius took her into his arms and kissed her. Jess tried to pull away but he held her firm, his tongue pushing between her lips and exploring her mouth. His kisses were so different than Rob, who even after 15 years of marriage still kissed her softly, almost tentatively. Darius kissed her roughly, like he owned her, forcing his tongue down her throat, wrapping his fingers in her hair so she couldn't pull away.

"No, stop, I'm married," Jess managed to say.

"I don't care," he said, and reached between them and cupped her right breast. Even through her bra and blouse he found her hard nipple, and roughly rubbed it with his thumb as he continued to kiss her. Jess moaned into his mouth. With his other hand at her back, he pulled her into him, pressing her against his crotch.

Jess found herself giving in. Necking with someone she just met was so slutty, so different from married life, and it excited her. She hadn't felt so free in a long time, not since being single. Darius was rough and aggressive, and it turned her on, and acting so bad in a public place added to the excitement. Also, in the back of her head, she knew this was what Rob wanted. Jess stopped struggling and kissed Darius back.

Then Jess felt Darius pull up her skirt. She felt his hand between her legs.

"Ugh god," she moaned into his mouth, as she felt him cup her mound. "Wait, stop, please."

"It's okay babe," Darius whispered into her ear, as his fingers stroked the camel toe formed in her pantyhose. "I just want to make you cum, that's all."

OH GOD! And he *WAS* going to make her cum too! His fingers felt *SO GOOD!*

But Jess didn't trust his assurances, she knew he'd want more, and if she didn't stop him soon she wouldn't be able to resist him.

"Please stop," Jess pleaded, pushing Darius away with both hands.

Darius stopped rubbing her pussy but continued to hold her firmly with an arm around her waist.

"Come on, what's the matter?" Darius said, clearly annoyed. "You're not just a cock tease, are you?"

"No, I mean ... I'm sorry," Jess stammered, still panting and trying to catch her breath as she pulled down her skirt. "It's just ... I haven't done this before. I mean ... not since I've been married."

Darius's expression softened. "That's cool, I understand. Do you want to go back to my place?"

Jess couldn't help smiling at Darius's boyish, single mindedness. "I'm married, remember? Going to your place wouldn't be the smartest thing I've ever done."

The 25-year-old shrugged. "My life has been a series of things I shouldn't have done," he joked.

That made Jess laugh. She stroked his cheek. "You're sweet, but I better be getting home."

"Come on, you can't leave me like this," he said, pointing to the tent in his pants.

Jess laughed again. She was taken by Darius's boyish charm, and was enjoying flirting with him. With a twinkle in her eye, she said "Well, the night's still young, you might meet someone else. Hopefully, someone who's not married this time? And, if you don't ... well, you've got a hand, right?"

Darius shot back a lecherous grin. He said, "Yeah, well, with the package I'm sporting, I'll need *both* my hands. And anyway, I prefer married girls. I like showing them what they're missing."

Jess gawked at Darius. "Oh my god, I can't believe you just said that!"

"Just telling the truth," Darius said with a confident grin. "And hey, I'm popular with married chicks. I'm Mr. No-Drama-Fun."

Jess punched him playfully in the ribs. "Well, Mr. No-Drama-Fun, not with this married chick. And anyways, the drama starts when girls you sleep with go home to their husbands. Now, I really have to get going." She reached up on her tip toes in her sensible 2-inch pumps and kissed him on the cheek. "Bye, I had fun. Um ... sorta ... I guess."

With a laugh, Jess turned and walked away.

CHAPTER 6

The phone rang, waking Jess. She was still sleepy, tired from all the drinks the night before (she was probably a little hung over too), and also because Rob had kept her up, fucking her like a wild man as she told him what happened.

"Hello?" she said into the telephone.

"You bitch!"

Jess winced at the shout in her ear. "Good morning Tina," she said.calmly.

"Don't good morning me!" Tina growled. "God, I can't believe you hooked up with Darius last night. I'm *so* jealous! Do you know how long I've wanted that teenage hunk?"

"He's not a teenager. He's 25," Jess said.

"I can dream, can't I?"

"God ....," Jess sighed.

"So tell me everything!" Tina demanded. "Does he fuck as good as he looks?"

"Nothing happened, not really. Anyways, he started it, not me."

"Oh, that makes me feel *sooooo* much better! God, I can't believe it! It's just like in college — and high school! You *ALWAYS* got the best-looking guys, even with your tiny tits! God, why did I start this? All the hot guys are gonna flock to you now, and I'll get all your leftovers!"

"I can't believe we're having this conversation. Are you *really* mad at me?"

"Yes, I am *REALLY* mad at you! And you're going to apologize by buying me lunch."

Jess didn't want to go to lunch. She wanted to go back to bed. "Um, I'm not sure I'm up for lunch today."

"After last night, you owe me lunch! And you're going to tell me every detail of what happened with Darius!" Then Tina slammed down the phone.

Jess rolled back into bed and hugged her pillow. All she wanted to do was take two aspirin and go back to sleep. Sighing, she threw back the covers. After telling Maria, their nanny, that she was going out for lunch, she went into the bathroom.

Jess paused to look in the mirror. Even after 15 years of marriage and 2 pregnancies, she was proud that her body was still firm. Her breasts were small, but they were still shapely and perky even after breastfeeding her two young children.

And Jess's legs — her best assets in addition to her pretty face — were still long and shapely. Her stomach was still mostly flat, and while she had gained weight around the hips, she liked it because it gave her some curves that she didn't have back in college.

Last night, Rob was all over her as soon as she got home. He fucked her twice and seemed to stay hard the entire time as she told him what happened, the dirty dancing with Tina, and her naughtiness with Darius. As they made love, he assured her over and over again that she had done exactly what he wanted her to do. He said, in fact, he wished she had gone farther with Darius.

Earlier that morning, with the good sense that a new day brings, Jess had worried Rob would be upset with her. But instead, Rob had awoken with a hard-on, and he fucked her again before he had to go to his office to get some things ready for a meeting he had on Monday.

She didn't know how she felt about Rob's fantasies, and this game they were playing. It was exciting, yes, but it wasn't something she expected to be doing when she took her wedding vows a little over 15 years ago. But then, husbands weren't supposed to encourage their wives to be with, and even have sex with, other men. So where did that leave her? Shaking her head, she stepped into the shower.

———◦———

"SO, HOW WAS DARIUS, and don't you dare leave anything out!" Tina demanded as soon as Jess sat down.

Jess told her. It was awkward at first. After all, she was married, and here she was talking about kissing and being fondled by another man. She still couldn't believe what happened last night. What she had done last night.

Tina leaned back in her chair as Jess finished. "Wow, I still can't believe it. You hooked up with Darius on your first try."

"We didn't hook up," Jess insisted.

"You sucked face, and he fingered you," Tina said. "That's hooking up, girlfriend."

Jess winced. She shook her head like she was trying to make last night go away. "I told you. It wasn't me. He followed me. He started it."

Tina scowled at her friend. "And I told you, you're not making me feel any better. Well, I guess I never had a chance. Darius must like flat-chested, leggy blondes, not voluptuous brunettes like me. So, what happened when you told your Robbie-boy?"

Jess shook her head. "He loved it. He was all over me. He said he wished I'd gone all the way with Darius."

"You're kidding?" Tina said incredulously. "Wow, I never would have believed it. Rob's so straight-laced. Well, I guess that answers the question. He really *does* want you to hook up with other guys. God, you're so lucky. Married to a great guy who's okay with you fucking other men."

"Will you keep your voice down!" Jess said, nervously glancing around to see if anyone had heard. "Anyways, what happened to *you* last night? I couldn't find you."

Tina broke into a wide grin. "Let me just say, if two is good, three is even better."

"You're kidding? You had three guys last night? God, you're such a slut!"

"And loving every minute of it, girlfriend! I feel like I'm at an all-you-can-eat buffet of stud-muffins! I'll take that one, and that, and a little of that too. It's all so easy! Being a girl is so easy to get boys!"

"Tina, you're the one being easy! You're giving them exactly what they want."

"Jess, I'm 38 and divorced. My ex was a shit, and I'm not ready to get into anything heavy right now. So, I think they're giving *me* exactly what *I* want. Ever time I'm getting fucked, I'm fucking over Chris. *And* his 20-year-old girlfriend. She's the real slut, getting a married man to cheat. Taking him away from his wife, his family."

Tina chocked out a sob as she wiped tears from her eyes. Despite whatever she said, she still wasn't over Chris. They had been the perfect couple. Their one child, their daughter, was even their combined namesake. Her name was Christina.

Jess reached over and squeezed her friend's hand. Tina wiped away the last tears and managed a grin.

"I'm having fun, Jess," Tina insisted. "Right now, I just want to be free. Have drama-less sex."

Jess was started by Tina's words. It reminded her of what Darius said last night. He was Mr. No-Drama-Fun.

Although Jess still thought of him as Mr. Tall-Dark-And-Handsome. She smiled at the thought.

Tina saw the smile. She knowingly said, "You're thinking about Darius, right?"

Jess blushed. Shit! She was 38, married with 2 kids, and she was blushing over a 25-year-old boy!

"Look," Tina said when it was clear Jess wasn't going to answer her question about Darius. "I'm 38. I still look good, but it won't last forever. So, I'm gonna kiss as many boys as I can. Maybe eventually I'll married me an older man who likes girls with big tits, and I'll be his trophy wife."

"I get it," Jess said. She and Tina were in different places in their lives. She had no right to judge her.

"You're so lucky, Jess," Tina said. "You've already got your older man. He follows you around like a puppy. You're he's trophy wife. And he gets off on the idea of you with other men. God Jess, you are so lucky."

"Robbie's not old," Jessie insisted.

"What's he, 45?" Tina scoffed with a skeptical laugh. "Don't get me wrong, he's a good man, a nice man. But he's not a stud muffin like those boys last night at the bar. Like Darius."

Jess shrugged. She knew Tina was right. Robbie *was* older. And while he was distinguished, it would be a stretch to call him handsome. But Robbie had character. He was kind, and steady, and a wonderful husband. A wonderful father. For all those reasons — and more — she loved Robbie.

That's why she was so concerned about Robbie's newly revealed fantasies, and the *fun* he wanted her to have. She wanted a normal life, a normal marriage, and a wife sleeping with other men certainly was not normal.

Tina read her friend's thoughts. She said, "Rob wants to see you with other men. You know, Darius is right, what he told you last night. A lot of the girls there, the ones wanting laid, they're married. So, who knows? You can't just assume they're cheating. Maybe their husbands are like Rob."

Jess looked skeptical. She didn't believe that for a second.

Tina saw the skeptical look on her friend's face. She said, "Look, Darius is incredibly hot, right? And you've seen the boys I've been with. They're all like ... like—."

"Young Greek gods?" Jess offered. The two girls giggled.

"Young Adonis's," Tina said back, and they giggled again.

Jess had to admit. It was fun talking to Tina like this. It was like they were in college again, when she was single and free. Before she met Rob and their relationship got serious.

Talking to Tina like this, Jess felt free, like she'd felt last night with Darius. She felt young and wild. It was exciting, thrilling even, to feel this way.

"You know I like Rob a lot. He's really nice. And he's good to you," Tina said.

Jessie frowned. She knew a *but* was coming.

"But honey, I've seen him in a bathing suit," Tina said. "And let's face it, he's no stud muffin down there. Never has been. Never will be. I mean, at 45, does he stay hard? Or does he need Viagra?"

Jessie gawked at Tina. "Did you really just say that to me? About my husband?" she said incredulously.

"You know what I mean. I just said I like Rob," Tina said. She lowered her voice, scanning the room to make sure no one was listening. "I'm just saying, if he's giving you a free pass with these gorgeous guys, I mean, if that's his fantasy, then god, *give him* his fantasy, make it come true!"

Jess thought of Darius, and her heart skipped a beat. He certainly matched the young Greek god description. If Rob wanted her to play out his fantasy with a young man like Darius ... the thought made her shiver, especially the *"young"* part – then why not give the man she loved what he wanted?

What would it be like, to have sex with a gorgeous man like Darius who was *13 years younger* than her? God! She *could* have been his babysitter!

"Well, maybe you're right," Jess hesitantly said.

"Of course, I'm right. I'm always right. I'm going out again tonight. Come with me."

Jess looked cross-eyed at her friend. She just had a *foursome* last night.

"God, Tina. You're insatiable."

Both girls laughed.

"Tonight's not good," Jess said. "We have to go to something. Rob's boss is having a party."

"Okay, next Friday, then."

Jess hesitated. "Well ... okay. Let me just check with Rob."

But she knew what his answer would be.

CHAPTER 7

LATER THAT NIGHT

"GUESS WHAT?" ROB SAID excitedly as they drove home from the party. "I think I might get that promotion."

"Really?" Jess said delightedly, grabbing her husband's arm. "Oh Robbie, that's wonderful! You've worked so hard for this! I'm so proud of you!"

"I shouldn't count my chickens before they're hatched, but I talked to Larry at the party, and he said I was the frontrunner. He said they'd decide by the end of the year. Larry said I need to work really hard between now and then, to really wow the C-suite." Larry was Rob's boss.

"I know they'll pick you!" she said excitedly, kissing her husband on the cheek. "You're so smart and wonderful!"

Rob felt great. With his beautiful wife beaming at him, so excited and proud of him, he felt like the luckiest man in the world.

"Um ... I think I might have a gift for you, kinda an early way to celebrate. Tina asked me to go out with her again next weekend. I said I would, if you're okay with it."

"Really?" Rob said excitedly. "Of course I'm okay with it! So you like this game too! I knew you would!"

"Yeah, I did have fun last night. More fun than I thought I would. It's a dangerous game, but exciting, just like you said it would be. As long as you're sure this won't hurt our marriage ...."

"It won't!" Rob assured her. "If anything, it'll make our marriage even better!" He pressed harder on the gas. "I can't wait to get home. I'm gonna fuck you all night long!"

CHAPTER 8

A WEEK LATER

JESS SIPPED HER APPLETINI and scanned the crowd.

"Looking for Darius?" Tina asked. She laughed when she saw her friend blush. "Don't be embarrassed, I don't blame you, I told you I've wanted him from the moment I laid eyes on his hot body. But he and his friends bar hop, I only see him every other week or so. But don't worry, I've been here before, they'll be tons of other hot guys. Hot *young* guys."

Jess soon found that Tina was right, and she had fun flirting and dancing with what seemed like an endless stream of young, gorgeous guys. Jess surprised herself at how easy she settled into the singles bar scene. It was so different from married life, and from being a mom. She loved Rob and their two kids, but this was so much fun. She felt like she was in college again. She had forgotten how much she loved dancing and flirting, and how exciting it was to be the attention of so many good-looking men.

Some of the guys were even as good looking as Darius. Well, almost. Tina sure knew the best places to go. But Jess didn't let anyone get as intimate as Darius. She let one or two boys get a little touchy-feely on the dance floor, and she even let one especially cute guy kiss her. She was tempted to let things go farther – she couldn't help it, there were so many hunky guys hitting on her—but decided not to.

She needed boundaries to Rob's *fun*. Flirting and dancing, a little touching, a little kissing ... and then she'll go home, tell Rob all about it, and let him fuck her brains out. She was happy with herself when she left the club, having decided she had struck a good balance between excitement and good sense.

As she predicted, Rob had worked himself into a frenzy fantasizing about what she was doing at the club. He actually took her from behind over the kitchen table within moments of her getting home – they'd never done that before—and then he did her twice more in their bed as she told him about all the flirting she had done. Rob was fucking Jess's brains out. The married couple was having more sex than ever before.

They feel asleep with Rob spooning Jess. She felt sexually satisfied and emotionally content with her marriage and her life with Rob. Her last thought before drifting off to sleep was, "Maybe Robbie's right. Maybe playing this game *will* make our marriage better."

CHAPTER 9

"Hi guys, this is Tony," Tina said as she approached the table with her new boy toy, a handsome twenty-something aspiring artist she met a week ago at a party. Rob had to suppress a grin. Nowadays, Tina always had a new younger man with her whenever they went out on a double date.

"Hey, nice to meet you," Tony said as he folded his tall, lean body into the chair facing Jess. Rob noticed that Tony's eyes lingered a moment too long on Jess. He couldn't blame him, Jess looked really good tonight. She wore one of his favorite outfits—a form-fitting, off-the-shoulder blouse, short black skirt, and black pantyhose. On her feet, Jess wore the sensible low-heeled pumps she often wore. Rob wished she would wear real stockings and stiletto high heels like Tina, but he knew his church-going, good girl wife could only take so much change.

Rob shook Tony's hand. Then Tony offered his hand to Jess. As he did with his eyes, Tony held Jess's hand a moment too long. Jess finally pulled her hand away. She glanced at Tina, blushed, then demurely looked down at her lap. Tina noted Tony's obvious attraction for her friend and Jess's discomfort with an amused expression on her face.

"Tony, come buy me a drink," Tina said, pulling her new boy-toy to his feet. "We'll be right back," she said over her shoulder as she walked with Tony to the bar.

"I see you like my friend Jess, you can't take your eyes off her," Tina said to Tony at the bar. She looked admiringly – and maybe a bit enviously—at Jess across the room. "I don't blame you, she looks really hot tonight."

Tina saw Tony's look of alarm and smiled. "Don't worry, I'm not jealous. Jess and I are really good friends." With a sly smile, then added, "Maybe someday I'll share you with her."

Tony gulped and his eyes grew wide. "You're kidding, right? A couple swap? That'd be great, but what're you going to do with Rob? He doesn't look your type."

Tina smiled mysteriously. "You never know. Anyways, it doesn't matter. It wouldn't be a swap. Rob likes the idea of his wife fucking other men."

Tony's jaw dropped, making Tina giggle. "She hasn't really done it yet … screw another guy, I mean. Rob wants her to, and he's pressuring her to do it. Maybe if you play your cards right, you might get lucky tonight."

Tony eyed her warily. "And you won't mind?"

Tina giggled again. "Are you kidding? I'd love it!"

Returning to the table, Tina made a point of sitting next to Rob, clearing the way for Tony to sit next to Jess. As Tony slid into the booth next to Rob's pretty wife, Tina smiled and winked at him.

As they talked and drank wine, Rob noticed how Tony edged closer to Jess in the booth. Jess seemed to be enjoying her conversation with the younger man. The bar was so loud they had to almost touch to hear each other. "Hey, let's dance!" Tony said.

"I'm game, I love this song!" Jess said enthusiastically.

"Nah, my new shoes are killing me," Tina said.

Jess looked over at her husband. "You guys go ahead," Rob said eagerly. He wanted to see his pretty wife dancing with this handsome young man.

Tony took Jess's hand and led her to the dance floor. Jess looked back at her husband, who winked at her. It was a slow song. Remembering what Tina had said, he pulled Jess close, wrapping his arms around her. Jess looked questioningly at Rob. Excitement covered his face. Seeing him nod encouragingly, she put her arms around Tony's neck.

Rob grew hard, watching his wife dancing with the younger, handsome man. They weren't dirty dancing, but Tony held Jess close, his chest almost touching her breasts. He wondered if Tony was hard, and whether Jess could feel his erection. The possibility made him lightheaded.

Tina's voice in his ear made him jump. He had forgotten she was there. "I'm sorry, what did you say?" he asked.

Tina smiled, a mischievous glint in her eye. "I said, you really like watching Jess with other men, don't you?"

Tina's question took Rob by surprise. "Well, ah, that is, ah ...," Rob stammered, his face growing red from embarrassment.

Tina jabbed him playfully in the ribs. "Don't be embarrassed. I think it's incredibly hot."

"You do?" Rob asked, genuinely surprised.

"Yeah, I do. I think it's really hot."

The music changed, and Rob looked back at his wife. It was a fast song, but they still danced slow. Tony had pulled her closer, pressing their bodies together. One of Tony's hands rested on Jess's shoulder, caressing the bare skin above her strapless top. His other hand rested on the small of her back, his fingers on her skirt, his thumb on her blouse.

Rob noticed the little things. The way Jess sometimes had to extend on her tip-toes to stay with the much taller man, the act causing her pretty feet to arch out of her pumps, and also causing her skirt to hike up, exposing more of her long legs. The flirty way Jess sometimes ran her fingers over Tony's muscular arms as they danced.

Rob wondered again whether Jess could feel Tony's erection. A lump formed in his throat as he realized that Jess hadn't danced so intimately with another man since before they started going out, over 15 years ago. He felt a sudden flash of jealousy, and had the urge to rush over and take his wife away from the younger man. But god, it was so exciting to see Jess dancing so closely with another man!

Tina seemed to read Rob's mind. "They look good together, don't they? Are you thinking about how they'd look in bed, naked, with Tony on top of your pretty wife?"

Tina's words were like gasoline on a fire, increasing Rob's lustful desires. "It doesn't matter. I don't think she'll go that far."

"I don't know about that," Tina said with a knowing grin. "I think she wants to. She just needs to be certain you'll be okay with it."

"I've told her already. What else can I do?"

Tina smiled. "I've got an idea."

———— ◆ ————

THE DJ BEGAN PLAYING fast songs, and another couple barreled into Jess and Tony. Her heart was pounding in her chest, and her body was tingling, from dancing with the handsome young man. She felt moisture between her legs. But she was concerned that Tina might be mad that she was dancing so intimately with her new boyfriend.

"Um, thanks for the dance, but we better get back."

"Where's Rob?" Jess asked when she got to the table.

"He left," Tina said.

"He left?" Jess said, shock and concern in her voice. "Is he mad?"

"No, he's not mad." Tina took Jess's hand and led her to a quiet corner. "He told me to give you this," she said, handing Jess a note.

Jess read the note:

"Jess, I really want you to go the next step. I can tell you want to do this too. But I sense it may be hard for you to do this if I'm there, so I've gone home. I hope you'll fulfill my fantasy. I think this is your fantasy too. If you do sleep with Tony, don't clean yourself up, just come home, I'll be waiting. I love you – Rob"

Jess slowly lowered the note, shock on her face. "I can't believe it. He really wants me to go all the way."

Tina shrugged. "I told you so. That's all he talked about while you and Tony were dancing. He was practically panting. He wants it to happen. I told him I don't care if you do it with Tony, he and I are just fuck-buddies, we're not serious."

Jess couldn't take her eyes off her husband's note. "What does he mean by not cleaning up?"

Tina smiled. "He said he wants to see you freshly fucked."

"What? That's what he said?"

"Those were his exact words – freshly fucked." Tina laughed. "God, Jess, I never knew Rob was so kinky!"

"Neither did I," Jess lamented, shaking her head. "So, what should I do?"

"That's so obvious. You should come back to my house, and let Tony fuck your brains out. Don't look at me like that. You know you want to. You were practically humping his leg out there. And trust me, Tony is really good, you'll love it. Rob's okay with it. He's *more* than okay, he *wants* you to do it, he's *begging* you to do it. So what are you waiting for?"

"What AM I waiting for?" Jess thought to herself. *"Rob wants me to do this. Why shouldn't I? Why should Tina have all the fun? Rob's okay with his wife with another man. So it wouldn't be cheating. I'd be giving Rob exactly what he wants. And yes, I admit, I want this too."*

"Okay," Jess said as she made her decision. "Let's go to your house."

CHAPTER 10

Rob sat in the basement of Tina's house, in what Tina called the video room. In the restaurant before he left, Tina told him her ex-husband Chris had installed video cameras throughout their house. Chris liked to video people having sex.

Tina swore Rob to secrecy, even Jess didn't know. Tina didn't want this to become public (especially because she couldn't stop Chris from keeping the sex tapes). She was afraid of becoming an outcast among her family and friends.

Tina got the house in the divorce settlement. She didn't use the video equipment anymore, but this seemed like the perfect way to help Rob achieve his fantasy. Jess would feel more comfortable being with Tony if she thought Rob wasn't watching. Unbeknownst to Jess, Rob could watch all the action from the video room. Tina told him he could even record it if he wanted.

Rob watched the front door open. Tina and Jess walked in, unsteady in their heels and giggling. Clearly they were feeling no pain from all the alcohol. Rob later learned they had shared two bottles of wine on the way home (in addition to the martinis at the restaurant). Tony was in the middle, an arm around each girl. Rob's pulse quickened seeing another man's arm around his wife.

They moved from the foyer to the living room, and Rob quickly pressed the button to shift to the living room camera. It was easy, all the buttons were labeled on the control panel, and he could zoom and pan. Chris also installed high end microphones. Tina promised Rob he would be able to hear every word, even whispers. And no one could hear him; the video room was soundproof.

"Come on, finish the story," Tony urged with a grin. "Tell me the other things you two did in college."

"Down boy, down!" Tina said, still giggling. She handed Tony a beer and poured wine for herself and Jess. "Stop panting on my sofa, I just had it cleaned!"

Jess laughed. "Anyways, why does it matter?" she asked, downing her wine in a single gulp and holding her glass out for more. Rob hadn't seen his wife so drunk in a long time. He watched her take another big gulp of wine. "That was so long ago."

"Then tell me when you lost your virginity," Tony asked Jess.

"Not going there," Jess said with a laugh.

"My first time, I smashed by best friend's mom," Tony said proudly. "Seduced her out of her pants."

Jess's lips parted in shock. "That's pretty bad," she said judgmentally, but her face showed she was intrigued, and maybe even impressed.

"Jess, you're one to judge," Tina said. "You've done some bad things yourself!"

The life-long friends shared a look, like they were remembering things from their past. A cloud seemed to pass between them, but it quickly passed.

Oblivious to the silent communication between the two girls, Tony shook his head. "I don't believe it. I can tell by looking at you. You're not a bad girl, you're too goody-goody."

"Uh oh, Jess, I think he's challenging you," Tina said, laughing.

Jess smiled at Tina, a twinkle in her eye. She took another sip of her wine, then put the glass down. She looked back at Tony, a sly smile on her face. She slowly leaned back into the chair and crossed her legs. Her short skirt hiked up her thighs, exposing most of her long shapely legs. Jess tilted her head slightly so her hair fell across her face. Then, with heavy lidded eyes looking through strands of her silky blonde hair, and in a sensuous Marilyn Monroe voice, she said, "Oh, Tony-Tony, you have no idea how bad I can be."

Rob gasped at his wife's performance. He had never seen her like this, acting the role of the seductress, acting so boldly. Is this how she used to act before they met? It was hard to believe this shameless flirt was the same sweet, church going girl he had married 15 years ago, and who was the mother of his two children. And what were they talking about, the bad things Jess had done in her past, that was even worse that Tony getting his best friend's mom to cheat on her husband?

Tony grinned lecherously at Jess, impressed with her performance. The pretty blonde excited him more than any girl in a long time. He was a leg man, and her long legs were incredible. That, combined with her pretty face really excited him.

Tony liked fucking married women, and it was even better because her husband Rob knew about it. Tina had told him Rob was a successful businessman, so it would give him alpha-dog pleasure to fuck his wife. Not wanting to wait further, he finished his beer, took off his shirt and walked towards the pretty blonde wife.

Jess looked alarmed – like a deer caught in the headlights—as Tony approached. She wasn't ready for the flirting to turn into reality. Seeing this, Tina quickly stood and intercepted him.

Tina said, "Slow down cowboy, you belong to me, I haven't decided if I'm going to give Jess a turn." Tina sat Tony down on the opposite sofa and nuzzled next to him. With the high quality audio gear, Rob heard Tina whisper into Tony's ear, "Slow down, or you'll scare her off."

Tina ran her hands over Tony's muscular chest. "God Jess, isn't he gorgeous?" she said as she used her fingertips to trace along the 20-something man's well-defined pecs and abs. Tina kissed Tony and he eagerly responded, and soon they were making out and heavily petting each other. Tina made sure not to block her friend's view of Tony's crotch, which by now had formed a huge tent in his pants.

Tony pushed Tina onto her back and pushed up her skirt. He spread her legs and moved his mouth to her pussy. The pretty MILF brunette wasn't wearing panties. She typically didn't wear any panties on dates with these young men, and she wore thigh highs instead of pantyhose. She wanted her boy-toys to have easy access to her most intimate girl parts.

"Oh gaaaawd," Tina groaned as Tony's tongue touched her clit. "Oh Jess, he's sooooo good at this."

Rob zoomed in on Tina's pussy as Tony licked it. His wife's BFF was completely hairless down there, like a porn star, and the sight made him shiver with lust.

But Rob was interested in Jess, not Tina. So he panned over to his wife.

Jess's eyes had an intense, aroused look to them as she watched Tina with her young lover. She was breathing hard, her nipples forming dents in her top. As if desiring physical stimulation, but too shy to openly play with herself, she rubbed her thighs back and forth. Rob's breath caught in his throat as he heard the swish-swish sound of her nylons rubbing together. Finally, needing more, and with her inhibitions lowered, Jess reached a hand into her skirt. Rob did the same, pulling his hard dick from his pants.

Tina suddenly grabbed Tony's hair and urgently pulled his face against her pussy. "Oh god!" she moaned as her body convulsed into a long orgasm. She lay on the sofa, catching her breath, and finally looked over to her friend and smiled. "Oh honey, you don't need to do that, Tony will take care of you, won't you Tony?"

Tony leered at Jess. His cock got even harder as he saw the sweet looking blonde with her hand down her skirt. The sight was so hot!

"It'll be my pleasure," he said, standing up and wiping Tina's pussy juices from his mouth. He walked over to Jess. This time she didn't pull away. His heavily muscled chest excited her. Then her eyes locked on the huge bulge in his pants.

As if reading her friend's mind, Tina said, "Jess, take off Tony's pants." She looked directly into one of the hidden cameras, so Rob felt like she was talking to him. She smiled wickedly. "You won't believe how big he is."

Jess's hands were quivering as she reached towards Tony's pants. She unbuckled his belt, and then undid the snap. "Hold on, hold on," Tony said. "Rub me first."

Jess looked at Tina as if asking for permission. *May I touch your lover?* Seeing Tina nod encouragingly, she cupped his crotch. Her small hand covered just a portion of the huge bulge. She slowly rubbed him through his pants, following the outline of his shaft.

Rob couldn't believe his wife was fondling another man's cock. He got lightheaded as the diamonds of her wedding and engagement rings sparkled as her left hand ran up and down Tony's shaft.

Jess was mesmerized. He felt so big and hard, even through the heavy fabric of his Levi's. She couldn't believe it when Tony grew even bigger. Abruptly she pulled her hands away, like she had been touching a hot stove.

"I can't believe I'm doing this," Jess said, laughing nervously.

"It's okay, Rob wants you to, remember his note," Tina quickly assured her.

Tony reached down and cupped Jess's breast over her blouse. Jess was so intent on Tony's crotch she didn't seem to notice.

Jess tried to unzip Tony's jeans, but she couldn't get the zipper over the huge hump formed by his erection. After two tries she again laughed nervously. "God, I'm so out of practice," she said embarrassed.

Tony grinned. He stood up and reached for his zipper. "I'll do it."

Rob held his breath as he heard the familiar sound of a zipper being pulled opened.

Jess grasped the waistband of Tony's unzipped jeans and pulled them down. His boxers sported a huge tent, but because the boxers were loose fitting, she couldn't discern much details. Her passion-fueled curiosity was killing her! Biting her lip, she hooked her fingers in the waistband, and pulled down his boxers.

"Oh my," Jess said, her eyes growing wide. She knew he was big but wasn't prepared for this.

Tony grinned proudly. He liked the effect his body had on women, especially pretty ones like Jess. "Go ahead, hold it," he urged her.

Mesmerized, Jess wrapped her hands around it. The shaft was so thick she couldn't fully wrap her hands around it, and so long she couldn't hold the entire length, even with one hand on top of the other. It was rock hard, yet the skin was so soft. She had an immense urge to kiss and lick it.

"I can't believe I'm doing this!" Jess said repeating her earlier disbelief. She blushed and covered her face with her hands.

Tina saw her friend needed some more motivation. "Tony, back in college, Jess had the reputation of giving great head. I think she's overrated, though," she taunted. "I'm a lot better than her."

Jess knew what Tina was doing. Still, her friend's mock challenge helped to lighten the moment. She remembered the fun they had back in college, and also her husband's note. Making a decision, she narrowed her eyes at Tina, and pretended to scoff, but couldn't completely hide her smile. "I'll guess we'll let Tony decide, won't we?"

"I guess so," Tina said smiling, knowing her friend's last inhibitions had just fallen.

Feeling like a co-ed again, Jess playfully stuck her tongue out at Tina, then scooted to the edge of the sofa with Tony standing in front of her. She kissed the head of Tony's cock, and then the shaft. Encouraged by Tony's moans, she raised his cock so it pointed upwards, then licked the sensitive underside of the long shaft, once again causing Tony to moan.

Rob excitedly stroked himself as he watched the action. Tony's size excited him. In all his fantasies, the men his wife fucked had huge cocks. Rob was noticeably smaller than Tony. By inches! For reasons he couldn't explain, the unfavorable comparison turned him on.

Rob shifted to a camera with a side view. Jess was still completely dressed, sitting with her ass on the edge of the sofa. She was holding Tony's shaft with both hands. She parted her lips wide and took him into her mouth. Rob groaned at seeing another man's cock in his wife's mouth for the first time. He had never seen a more erotic sight.

Jess let Tony's cock slip from her lips. She moved off the sofa and got on her knees, with the young man taking a step back to make room for the sexy blonde MILF. Then, she pushed his pants and boxers all the way down before slowly kissing and licking his rod up and down until reaching his balls. She gently and thoroughly licked and sucked each one. Wanting to impress the young gorgeous man, she moved her pretty face between his open legs. Then reaching up, she softly licked his sandbar, and then gently flicked the tip of her tongue over his rectum.

"Oh fuck, that's good!" Tony moaned.

Tony's compliment thrilled her. Encouraged, she flicked at his cockhead where pre-cum had formed. She let a thin thread of his pre-cum trail from his cockhead to her lips. She let the pre-cum thread hang for a few seconds, then expertly twined it around her tongue and swallowed it. She did all this while looking at Tony's face with her sweet, big blue eyes.

Tony's cock pulsed excitedly at the sight. "Fuck that's nasty!" he hissed. "You're a bad girl, aren't you?"

Jess's eyes were glazed over with lust. She licked the remaining pre-cum off Tony's cockhead, and then rubbed the bulbous head across her face. "Yeah," she said huskily. "I'm a bad girl."

Tony marveled at the pretty blonde kneeling in front of him. He couldn't believe this sweet looking girl was such a slut. He reached behind her and expertly unzipped her blouse. He pulled it off and tossed it onto the floor.

Then he pushed Jess back a bit, creating space between the two of them. He hooked a finger in the thin material connecting the cups of her strapless bra, and pulled down, exposing her breasts. "I've wanted to see your tits all night long," he said, leering at her. He cupped both breasts and roughly rubbed the hard upturned nipples.

Jess grimaced at the sudden pain but didn't protest. He lowered his head and sucked on her nipples, biting hard. While grimacing again, her tight body also writhed with pleasure. That pleased Tony. He liked a little rough play, and saw Jess liked it too.

Tina came over and knelt next to Jess. "Here, let me help you with this," she said, reaching behind Jess's back and unsnapping her bra. Tina pulled the bra off and tossed it onto the floor next to Jess's blouse.

Then her hands went to Jess's skirt. "Honey, raise up a little." Jess did as her best friend asked and raised her hips. Tina quickly unzipped Jess's skirt and tugged at the waist. The skirt wouldn't move, because it was tight, and despite her slimness, Jess did have some curves.

"Help me Tony," Tina said, and the powerful Tony easily pulled the mini-skirt down Jess's legs. In a moment it was lying on the floor next to Jess's blouse and bra.

Tina gripped the waistband of Jess's pantyhose and pulled down, at the same time pulling off her panties. She struggled a bit with the pantyhose, like with the skirt. "Honey, you need to wear thigh highs. Boys love it, and it makes it easier for them to get to your fun parts."

Tina took off Jess's pumps, then finished removing the pantyhose and panties.

"Honey, let's put these back on, guys really like that, don't they Tony?"

"Oh yeah, we love it!" Tony said.

With a shaky left hand, Rob zoomed on Tina putting the black pumps on Jess's feet (his right hand was around his dick, slowly pumping up and down). He wished they were stiletto *fuck-me* pumps, but these 2" heels still looked good on his wife's shapely long legs.

Jess looked incredibly sexy, completely nude except for the black pumps. Rob heard the heels scrap against the wood floor as Tony gently pushed her legs apart. He panned back so he could see their entire bodies.

Tony lowered his face to Jess's pussy. He liked what he saw. Her pussy was smooth and tight, with lips that were thin and just a shade darker than the surrounding skin. He was a little surprised she wasn't hairless. She was trimmed but not bare. Most of the cougars he fucked, like Tina, kept themselves completely hairless by getting regular Brazilians (at least that's what he assumed), and he (and his friends) preferred that. There was nothing better than seeing an older chick with a pussy as bare as a little girl's.

Then Tony remembered this was Jess's first time with another man, and inwardly smiled. He loved fucking other men's wives, there was a special thrill about taking a pussy that belonged to another man. And probably if Jess turned into a cock-slut like Tina, she'd get regular pussy and ass waxings like all the other cougars who craved young dick.

Beads of sweat formed on Rob's brow as he watched Tony's head disappear between his wife's thighs. A moment later he heard Jess moan, and he knew Tony's tongue had found her clit. Tony pushed her legs farther apart, giving him complete access to her pussy. He reached up and fondled her tits as he ate her. Jess clutched the sofa cushions, her back arching. "Ohhhh gawwwwwd," she groaned as her body convulsed in an orgasm.

Seeing another man make his wife cum was too much for Rob. His cock jerked and shot cum onto his chest as he came.

"Oh god" Jess gasped as her orgasm peaked, then slowly receded. Tony got up and wiped his mouth across the back of his hand.

Rob expected Tony to enter her immediately, but instead he moved up Jess's body and kissed her. Jess immediately returned Tony's kisses. For some reason, seeing his wife kiss Tony with such passion bothered Rob. In the emotional clarity that comes after an orgasm, Rob wondered if he had made a mistake, letting another man (especially a man as young and good looking as Tony) enjoy his wife's charms.

After several minutes of kissing, Tony pulled Jess to her feet. "Let's go upstairs."

"I'll join you guys in a minute," Tina said, smiling.

After they disappeared upstairs, Tina looked into the camera. "Rob, call me now if you want me to stop this from going any farther."

Conflicting emotions raged through Rob. Seeing his wife naked in front of another man, seeing them kiss and have oral sex, seeing the other man make her cum – it was exciting beyond belief – but also disturbing. Their marriage was wonderful, she was devoted to him, and now they'd brought another man into the equation. He felt a pain in his stomach (or was it his heart?). Yet, seeing the two of them just moments ago, the muscular man on top of his wife, kissing and fondling her, it was an incredible sight! His dick was already hard again. And seeing how Jess had acted with Tony – he had never known his wife was such a bad girl! He burned to see her fucked by Tony. He had never wanted anything more in his life.

Not hearing the telephone ring, Tina grinned into the camera. "You're so kinky, I love it!" She turned toward the stairs, then looked over her shoulder into the camera. "Are you coming?" she teased, giggling at the double entendre.

Rob switched to the camera in the guest bedroom. He was relieved to see they weren't fucking yet, because he wanted to watch his wife's face as Tony first penetrated her with his monster cock.

Jess lay on her back on the bed. She still wore the black heels. Tony was between her legs, which were bent at the knees, and spread wide to accommodate Tony's large muscular body.

Jess reached between their bodies and took hold of his cock. She rubbed his cockhead up and down between her pussy lips. It felt sooooo good. She desperately wanted to feel him inside her.

"Do you have a condom?" Tess asked Tony.

"Sorry babe. I'm empty," Tony said. Tess groaned with frustration.

Tess looked hopefully at Tina. "Do you have a condom?" she asked.

Tina shook her head. "You know I like skin on skin."

Jess frowned at her friend. *That's easy for you to say,* she thought. There was a complication when she gave birth to her only child, Christina, and now she wasn't able to have children any longer.

Tess looked back at Tony, who shrugged apologetically.

It was too late to stop now. Her body ached to feel Tony inside her. "Okay, just don't cum in me, okay?" Tess said.

Tony grinned, admiring her pretty face. "Sure. Can I cum on your face, babe?"

Jess giggled at his predictability. "Well, maybe if you're a good boy," she teased.

"Oh, I'm *very* good," he said as he leaned in and kissed her. As they French kissed, Jess again reached between their bodies and took hold of Tony's cock. She guided him towards her pussy.

"Just go slow," Jess breathed between kisses. "You're bigger than I'm used to."

Rob shuddered at his wife's unfavorable comparison of him to her new lover. And his head was exploding about Jess letting Tony inside her without a condom, even though she was unprotected. But Rob, like Tess, knew it was too late to stop. He wanted to see his wife getting fucked by this virile young man!

Rob shifted the screen to a split view, half of the screen on Jess's face, the other on her pussy.

"Oh god!" Jess groaned through clenched teeth as Tony penetrated her pussy with his bulbous cockhead. Her hands clutched the sheets. "I haven't – had – something—so big – in a long – time," she grunted between breaths as Tony penetrated her.

Rob's head was exploding again! His wife had another man's cock inside her!

Jess wasn't a virgin when they met. Neither was he. But for over 15 years, his cock was the only one inside her.

That was no longer true! Now Jess had another man's cock inside her!

Rob was breathing hard as he looked at his wife's face—her eyes clenched shut, her cheeks flushed, her nostrils flaring. His heart pounded at the sight of his wife's pussy being slowly penetrated by another man's cock.

"Yeah Tony, give it to her," he panted under his breath as he stroked his dick. His penis was much smaller than Tony's. "Push your thick cock into my wife's pussy. Let her see what a real cock feels like." Rob's self-degrading thoughts pushed him over the edge, and with a lurch he came again.

With his lust temporarily sated, Rob's misgivings returned. But he couldn't take his eyes off the screen. "God, oh god, oh god," he heard his wife moan as, inch by inch, Tony's cock disappeared inside her. "It feels so good!" Jess cried.

As Rob felt arousal stirring within him again as he watched his wife being penetrated by another man's cock, he felt another emotion he had never felt before. Self-loathing.

"There!" Tony said triumphantly. "It's all in you now, all 9 inches!" He began to slowly rock back and forth, pumping his cock in and out of Jess's married pussy.

"Oh god yes!" Jess moaned. "Fuck me, fuck me!"

Tony's pace quickened. "You want it hard, is that it?"

"Yes, yes!" Jess begged. "Fuck me hard!"

Tony lifted Jess's long legs over his shoulders, smashing her thighs against her tits, and pounded her.

"Oh god, oh god, oh god!" she cried, her hands gripping the sheets as if holding on for dear life. Then her body tensed and she came. "Ahh ahh ahh!" she moaned, wrapping her arms around Tony's neck. Tony leaned down and covered Jess's mouth with his own. Her manicured nails dug into Tony's muscular shoulders, her orgasm peaking with her young lover's tongue swirling in her mouth.

In the video room, the sight of Jess cumming on Tony's cock pushed Rob over the edge, and he came once again. He couldn't believe he had cum again so quickly.

Tony's pace slowed, but didn't stop, the gentle rocking helping Jess extend the pleasure of her orgasm. He released Jess's legs from his shoulders, and they fell back to the bed, bent at the knee, her heels flat on the bed. During this time, as Jess's orgasm peaked and gradually faded,

Tony kept his lips locked on Jess's, gently kissing her and exploring her tongue with his own. Gradually he quickened his pace, but their fucking was not as frantic as before. Tony rotated his hips, searching for Jess's g-spot. He knew he had found it when she moaned from the pleasure, and then he focused his cock on that magical spot inside her, making sure to rub it with each stroke. At the same time, Tony leaned into Jess so as to rub the shaft of his cock against her clitoris, back and forth, over and over, expertly stimulating both her g-spot and clit.

"Oh god, that feels good, yeah, yeah, just like that. God, oh god, you're going to make me cum again," Jess moaned as she felt another orgasm building inside her, which surprised her since she had already cum twice.

Rob sat disheartened as he watched Tony bring his wife to the brink of another orgasm. His cock lay limp in his hand, his lust sated for the moment. "God, god, I'm cumming!" he heard his wife cry, her body convulsing as she once again orgasmed in another man's arms. Rob imagined his wife's pretty toes curling inside her pumps, and his cock twitched to life.

"That felt so good, you're incredible," Jess gasped between breaths, marveling at the intensity of pleasure she had just experienced. She finally caught her breath. "Here, roll over," she said to Tony, knowing he hadn't cum yet. On top, Jess moved on his shaft, riding him up and down. She squeezed her pussy muscles on each downward stroke to increase his pleasure. She learned to do this years ago with Rob. She couldn't squeeze as hard with Tony's much larger member, but judging by his moans he liked what she was doing.

Jess leaned over and kissed Tony, then worked down from his mouth to his neck, then up to his ear. As this was their first time together, she paid close attention to his reactions, sucking and licking when his body reacted, moving on when it didn't. She licked around his ear, then flicked her tongue into his ear.

"Ugh fuck!" Tony groaned immediately, his back arching so violently he almost tossed her off him.

Jess smiled inside, knowing she had found one of his erogenous zones. She lightly licked his ear again, probing for just the right pressure to pleasure him, at the same time continuing to move up and down on his thick shaft.

"Oh god baby you're good!" he said appreciatively, wrapping his arms around her neck and returning her kisses. They stayed like that for what seemed like minutes.

Rob's cock had returned to life, and he was lightly stroking himself. Seeing his wife work so hard to please Tony made him heartsick with jealousy, but it aroused him too. It was incredibly erotic to watch his wife straddling Tony, impaled on his long thick cock, her beautiful legs tensing as she fucked him. Once again, seeing her intimately kissing him, sometimes passionately, other times tenderly and even lovingly, was worse than watching them fuck, but it also turned him on in a masochistic sort of way.

"Oh fuck, I'm close to cumming!" Tony warned. The couple hurriedly changed positions, with Jess on her back, and Tony straddling her chest. Tony pointed his cock at Jess's pretty face, rapidly stroking himself. Wanting to give him as much pleasure as he gave her, she reached under him and lightly probed along his sandbar, and then pressed a finger against his rectum.

"OHHH FUCK!" he growled at the sudden intense pleasure, and then he came. Waves after waves of his thick cum shot from his cock and landed on her cheeks and chin, into her open mouth, over her eyes, and in her blonde hair.

When he was done, Jess's face was coated with his cum. She held her hands to the side in a helpless gesture and started to laugh. "Oh god, that's a lot," she said marveling at the amount of Tony's ejaculation.

"Here," Tina said helpfully, handing Jess a towel. Jess wiped her face. "Don't wipe it all off," Tina said mischievously. "Remember Rob wants to see you freshly fucked."

Rob saw his wife roll her eyes, and then the two girls laughed. It was like a stake through his heart.

"I better get home to my husband," Tess said, sliding out of bed. Suddenly feeling modest, she covered her naked body with a sheet. She picked up her blouse and skirt and headed for the hallway, intending to dress in Tina's bathroom.

Tony gently grabbed her hand. "Can I see you again?"

Jess hesitated, not knowing what to say. She had enjoyed being with Tony immensely, but she was married after all. "I'm not sure," she answered honestly.

Jess got dressed and left for home. Rob had already left, Tina knew. The video room was empty when she checked a moment ago.

Soiled tissues were in the trash can. Tissues used by Rob to clean himself after cumming. There were multiple balls of tissues, each one representing a Rob orgasm. Tina laughed and said to herself, "God Rob, how many times did you cum watching your sweet Tess getting fucked?"

Tina picked up one ball of tissues and took a sniff. She grinned and said to herself, "You don't smell half bad, Robbie."

CHAPTER 11

Rob grabbed Jess's hand as soon as she got home in the taxi, and rushed her up to their bedroom. He had driven like a madman to beat her home, all the while reliving what he had seen from Tina's video room. He was hard again, even though he had already cum multiple times that evening.

Rob closed the bedroom door and then stepped away from his wife. "Just stand there for a minute. I want to look at you."

Jess looked quizzically at her husband, and then understood. She smiled impishly. "Do you like how I look?"

Rob studied his wife. She wore the same blouse and skirt, but she hadn't bothered to put back on her bra or pantyhose. Also, her lip stick was long gone, and her hair was disheveled and a matted in places (from Tony's dried cum?).

"Yeah, I do, I think you look great," Rob finally replied. He pulled his wife to him, and covered her mouth with his. His hands roamed over her body. She *did* look freshly fucked, and it made him lightheaded with excitement. He was sure he could smell Tony on her. He pushed her onto the bed and pushed up her skirt. She hadn't bothered to put back on her panties either, and when he spread her legs he saw that her pussy lips were still swollen. He got between her legs and pulled down her blouse. Her normally milky white breasts were red from the abuse they had taken from Tony's rough fondling. This further evidence of another man's use of his wife's body excited him more.

He pulled down his pants, and positioned himself between her legs. "Did he fuck you?" he asked, being careful not to let Jess know he had watched it all.

"That's what you wanted, isn't it?" she said guardedly.

"God yes!"

"Then, yeah, that's what he did. He fucked me."

"Oh god!" he moaned. He had watched it all, but it thrilled him to hear her say it. He pushed into her. Her pussy was hot and looser than normal. It had never felt so good. "Did he make you cum?"

"Yes."

"How many times?"

Jess hesitated as she thought back. "I can't remember," she said honestly. "A lot."

"Oh god," Rob groaned, his wife's words making him shudder with passion. "Was he good?"

"Yeah," she replied, certain now her husband wouldn't be upset by the truth. "He was really good."

Rob grunted as he came.

A few minutes later, they spooned in their king-size bed. Rob's thoughts returned to what he had witnessed in Tina's video room, and he started getting hard again. Jess felt him and giggled. "So soon?"

"I can't help it, just thinking about it makes me hard. So – are you going to do it again?"

Jess laughed. "I think I've had enough excitement tonight to last a lifetime," she insisted, but Rob sensed she didn't really mean it.

"Oh come on, admit it, you loved it, and so did I. Besides, there are so many more young studs for you to try out."

She laughed again. "Tina calls them the Stallions."

"The Stallions, huh? Don't you mean the milf-hunters?" They laughed. "Anyway, don't you think it would be fun to hang out with them, like Tina?"

"Just hang out?" she asked in a mischievous voice. She was teasing him now. "Or, *hang out like Tina?*"

Rob pulled his wife to him. "You know what I mean." He pushed into her. "Anything you do with them is okay with me. Anything."

CHAPTER 12

ONE MONTH LATER

ROB FOUND HIS WIFE already at the bar, sitting at a large table with Tina and three Stallions.

Jess was talking and laughing with Darius. "Hi honey," she said, affectionately squeezing his arm and kissing him on the cheek. She slid over to make room for him, but then went back to flirting with Darius. Tina smiled at Rob, but soon returned to flirting with the other two 20-something men. Rob felt awkward sitting at the table, like a third wheel. Tina said she wanted to dance and pulled the two guys with her. Darius and Jess laughed, and soon they both were up and heading to the dance floor.

Over the last month, Jess had partied with Tina and the Stallions every weekend. She seemed like a different person. She loved dancing and the club scene. It reminded Rob of college, when he first met her. One of the prettiest girls on campus, and always incredibly popular, she partied with Tina and her other sorority sisters all the time. As far as Rob knew, she never had a steady boyfriend until they started going out, instead dating a lot of guys. Even to this day, Rob couldn't believe she fell in love with him, being so different from the other guys she used to date. Now, though, it seemed she had returned to her college days, because the Stallions were just like those guys she used to date in college. They weren't much older than those guys either.

Rob wondered if Jess had slept with all those guys from college. If not, she certainly was doing her best to catch up. Over the last month, from Tina's video room, he had watched her in bed with 3 different Stallions.

Jess spent more time with Darius than any other Stallion. He was clearly her favorite. Rob had watched her have sex with him 4 times. He still hadn't told Jess about the video room, and as far as he could tell Tina hadn't said anything either. Rob liked watching his wife have sex with other men, and then come home later and tell him about it.

Rob felt awkward being there. In the hot wife stories he read, the husband usually watched his wife from the shadows of the bar. But that wasn't an option, because it quickly spread among the Stallions that Jess's husband liked to watch. While he felt awkward sitting at the Stallions' table, he would feel even more foolish hiding in the shadows, with them knowing he was there.

Rob didn't always go with Jess when she partied with Tina and the Stallions. Sometimes he'd stay home. Either way, though, he'd always sneak into Tina's video room. Tina had even given him a key so he could go through her basement door. Lucky for him – and Jess – their grandmotherly nanny, Maria, was live in so she was always there to watch the 2 kids.

When he did go, the Stallions mostly ignored him. They openly flirted with Jess in front of him. She devoted most of her attention to the Stallions, and didn't object when they fondled her right in front of her husband. This bothered Rob, of course, but thrilled him too.

Rob wasn't used to his wife paying so little attention to him. It hurt and made him jealous. But he was coming to understand that this was part of the game, and the thrill. Somehow, in a dark way, the hurt feelings and jealously worked to heighten his arousal. And there was no doubt he was aroused.

Tonight, Jess wore a short black dress that showed off her long shapely legs. He loved seeing her in it, and she looked so sexy dancing with Darius. He left the bar and headed to his car, eagerly anticipating what he might see later that night in Tina's video room.

And then once Jess got home, Rob would reclaim his wife. Even though Jess was fucking other men, the sex life of the married couple had never been better. They were having sex like they were newlyweds. And when she was home, Jess was her loving self and lavished attention on Rob. So, maybe what people said was true. The hot wife lifestyle actually *improved* the couple's marriage.

CHAPTER 13

TWO MONTHS LATER

ROB SAT AT THE DESK in his home office, trying to finish a project for work. Upstairs, Jess was getting ready to go out, another Friday night with Tina and the Stallions. He wanted to go, but he had too much work. He had gotten the promotion, and he and Jess enjoyed having the extra money, but he often had to bring work home to keep up.

Jess entered the den and kissed him on the cheek. "How do I look?"

"You look incredible!"

Jess wore her favorite skinny jeans. He loved the way she looked in them. They were made of really thin fabric, so they were almost like tights, showing every contour of her long, shapely legs. Jess had majored in ballet and modern dance in college – she still danced regularly in a local ballet studio—and it showed in her legs. While incredibly slim and shapely, her long legs were also lithe and muscular, and the skinny jeans showed the rippling of her leg muscles as she moved. They also really showed off her tight ass. Jess knew Rob loved seeing her in the jeans. It kind of bothered him that she had chosen to wear them tonight, when he wouldn't be able to go with her.

The doorbell rang. "That's Tina, I've got to go," she said excitedly. She gave Rob a quick peck on the cheek, and rushed out the door.

Rob had a hard time working, distracted by what Jess might be doing with the Stallions. For months she had partied almost every weekend with Tina and the Stallions. Most times she'd end the evening fucking Darius. That bothered him, because she had started going to Darius's apartment to fuck, so he couldn't watch from Tina's video room; he had to be satisfied with just their pillow talk when she got home. It also bothered him that she was spending so much time with Darius. It was almost like they were going steady, like she was Darius's girlfriend.

His computer buzzed, interrupting his thoughts. It was an email from Tina. He opened it: "Thought you'd like these."

Attached to the email were pictures. Suspecting what they might be, he eagerly opened the first picture. It was of Jess in the bar, looking great in her skinny jeans. Her tailored, crisp white blouse nicely showed off her petite body, and her stiletto heels made her already long legs look even longer. Yes, Jess had expanded her wardrobe to include multiple pairs of 4-inch, stiletto *fuck-me* heels. Gone were the sensible 2" pumps she used to wear. Jess still owed them and wore them to church, but she always wore the sexier stilettos when she partied with Tina and the Stallions.

Darius had his arm around his wife, and she was talking and laughing with him.

In the next picture, the Stallions had Jess bent over a pool table. She was still fully clothed and everyone was laughing, so it looked like they were just horsing around. Skin was showing between Jess's jeans and blouse. Her thong had crept up her back, and Darius was grinning lecherously into the camera, pretending to tongue the black lace of her thong.

Rob didn't understand the next picture. Jess was surrounded by the Stallions. They were all laughing. Darius was trying to get Jess to take something (it looked like a white towel), but Jess was laughing and shaking her head no.

Rob's eyes grew wide in shock at the next picture. Tina was standing next to Jess, both of them surrounded by the Stallions. Inside the circle, Tina had taken off her shirt and bra! Rob zoomed into Tina's chest. As he always suspected, she had great tits. They were large and shapely. Maybe they were beginning to sag a little bit – she was 38 after all, and had breast fed her daughter Christina—and she could stand to lose a few pounds around her stomach, but there was no doubt that Tina was a desirable woman. But the little sag in her big tits explained why Tina typically wore a bra, although sometimes she did go braless.

In the next picture, Tina had put on a tight t-shirt that scooped in the front, showing a lot of her cleavage. Now Rob got it. The club was having a wet t-shirt contest, and the Stallions were trying to get the girls to enter.

In the next picture, Rob saw two other girls topless, in the process of putting their t-shirts on. They were younger than Tina and, standing next to them, Tina looked like, well, a 38-year-old woman standing next to a couple of young 20-something girls. Their pretty faces looked younger, and both had tits as big as Tina's, but perkier with upturned nipples that seemed to point straight up to the ceiling.

Standing next to the younger girls, Tina wasn't nearly as pretty or desirable. Rob imagined the Stallions always had younger girls around them, and he wondered if the comparison bothered Tina. He wondered if Jess shared the same concerns.

The next picture again showed Jess in the middle of the circle. The Stallions were egging Jess to take off her top and put on the t-shirt. Darius had his arms around her, trying to unbutton her top. Jess was laughing, playfully slapping Darius's hand.

In the next picture, Darius had his arm around Jess's waist, smiling and whispering into her ear, clearly trying to convince her to enter the contest. Jess, an arm around Darius and the other holding his hand at her waist, seemed delighted with whatever Darius was saying to her, a big smile on her face. With a pang of jealousy, Rob couldn't help noticing how they looked like a couple. It looked like Darius and Jess were the couple, instead of him and Jess.

In the next picture, Jess had finally relented and taken off her blouse and bra but had impishly turned so her back faced the Stallions. She was looking back at them over her shoulder with a teasing smile, and the Stallions (including Darius) were booing.

But in the next picture, Jess had turned, revealing her topless body to the Stallions. It didn't really matter. Rob was sure by now most – if not all—of the Stallions had seen his wife's naked body, either at Tina's house or Darius's apartment.

In the picture, Jess stood next to Tina and the two younger girls. Like Jess, those two girls had not yet put on their t-shirts.

Unlike Tina, Jess looked really good next to the younger girls. Although probably 15 years older, Jess was naturally prettier than the two younger girls, and her soft blonde hair and big blue eyes gave her a fresh, innocent look that was lacking in the younger girls.

Jess couldn't compare size-wise in the tits department, but her breasts were as shapely and perky as the younger girls', and her smallish breasts gave her a younger girlish look that appealed to many men (like Rob). Also, unlike Tina, Jess's tummy was as flat and sexy as the younger girls.

What set Jess apart from the younger girls, and just about every other female on the planet, were her long shapely dancer's legs. In her form-fitting skinny jeans and high heels, and being nude from the waist up, she was breathtakingly beautiful and desirable. The younger girls weren't in her class, which was confirmed a few pictures later. That picture showed about 20 girls on stage, all of them in their t-shirts after being soaked with water (Tina wasn't on stage, so she must have bowed out of the contest and kept taking pictures). Jess was easily the prettiest girl on stage (even though she had the smallest tits by far). It didn't surprise Rob, then, that the next picture showed the MC giving Jess the winner's medal.

The next picture was actually a movie. The video was gritty because it was taken in low light. Tina later told Rob it was taken in the alley behind the bar. In the video, Jess was against the alley wall, sucking face with Darius. Darius moved his hand between their bodies and cupped her breast. Then he unbuttoned her jeans and pushed them down her legs. Jess kicked them off, somehow managing to keep her heels on, and then she reached down and almost frantically unzipped his jeans and pulled out his cock. Once again, Rob marveled at the size of Darius's cock. It was the longest and thickest he had ever seen, like John Holmes on steroids.

Because he was so much taller (even with Jess in her 4-inch-high heels), Darius had to bend at the knees to position himself. He thrust up violently, practically raising Jess out of her high heels. She moaned as his thick cock penetrated her. She wrapped her arms around his neck and her leg around his thigh, and Darius fucked her hard, each thrust pushing her hard against the wall. They fucked like wild animals, their lips locked together the entire time. As Rob excitedly masturbated to the video, he was reminded of the time when Tina had given a wall job to her then lover, Jason.

Rob watched his wife cum. He could always tell when she orgasmed, either by the look on her face, the way her back arched, or the curling of her toes. Darius seemed about to cum as well. Jess pulled away from him and got on her knees. That pleased Rob. At least she wasn't letting him cum inside her.

As she stroked and sucked on Darius, Rob's attention was brought to Jess's left hand. He frowned. She wasn't wearing her wedding and engagement rings. He paused the video and quickly scrolled through the earlier pictures. He hadn't noticed before, but she wasn't wearing her rings in any of the pictures.

Rob tried to remember earlier that evening. He was certain she had been wearing her rings then. She must have taken them off before meeting Darius. The realization made him heartsick. They hardly saw each other on weekends anymore. He saw her even less since getting the promotion, since he often had to work late or on weekends. Feelings of loneliness and jealousy washed over him.

Rob switched back to the video and hit play. Jess was on her knees, Darius's cock stuffed in her mouth. She still wore the wet t-shirt, but was nude from the waist down. The wet t-shirt was pasted against her body, her tits clearly outlined and visible through the translucent material. Darius gripped Jess's blonde hair, holding her head still as he fucked her pretty face. With each thrust he only went a few inches into her mouth – he was too thick to go farther – but Rob could tell his wife had to work hard to keep from gagging, and saliva rolled off her chin and down her neck.

Darius jerked Jess's hair hard as he came. She grimaced with pain, but didn't pull away. Her cheeks ballooned as Darius filled her mouth with cum. He was shooting his jism into her mouth faster than she could swallow. Then he pulled out, and took his cock in his hand. With his other hand still holding the back of her head, he shot a final load of his spunk onto her face. Jess didn't try to pull away. Instead, she tilted her head up and looked at him with her big blue eyes as he ejaculated.

After he finished cumming, Jess took his cock in both hands, and rubbed it across her face, spreading his cum all over her pretty face. Rob heard clapping and applause. Tina and the other Stallions – and maybe the entire bar – had seen the show.

Realizing they had an audience, Jess shyly looked away, reaching for her discarded jeans. Somehow, even though she had just been fucked in an alley, and with spunk all over her face, her demure reaction to the unwanted audience made her seem innocent, adding to her desirability and making her more alluring.

Hearing the applause, Darius initially had a big smile on this face and shook his first triumphantly at the crowd, like he was celebrating his conquest of this pretty married MILF. But then, realizing that Jess was upset, he scowled at the crowd and told them to fuck off. He helped Jess put on her jeans, positioning his large muscular body to shield her from the crowd.

While watching the video, Rob had cum twice. But as the video ended, with Darius's arm protectively around his wife, the pangs of jealousy and doubt returned.

CHAPTER 14

Jess got home around 3am. Tony dropped her off, not Darius, which surprised Rob. She still wore the skinny jeans and white blouse, but held the backs of the sexy high heels with two curved fingers of her right hand. Rob wondered where the t-shirt had ended up. Jess begged off any conversation, saying she was exhausted, and went right to sleep.

The next morning, Jess seemed distracted. She said she didn't sleep well. Rob thought she was probably hung over. Hung over or not, though, he needed to talk to her. He motioned at her left hand. "What happened to your rings?"

Jess didn't understand at first, but then she looked at her left hand and her eyes went wide. "Oh, god, sorry Robbie," she said as she reached for her purse. She retrieved her engagement and wedding rings from the zippered pouch and put them back on. She didn't offer any explanation, still seeming to be distracted. Then she saw Rob looking at her expectantly. He wanted to know about the rings.

"Honey, I'm sorry, but it was awkward," she explained. "People know Darius isn't married. Then they see me with him, and they see my rings, so then I have to explain why a married woman is with a single man. So, it's just easier to take off the rings."

Rob frowned. He said, "That's something else I want to talk about. It seems like you're with Darius a lot."

Jess shrugged, not understanding his point. "So? That's what you want, isn't it?"

"No, it isn't. The game is about you with other men, not *one particular* man. You're with Darius all the time. It's like you're dating him."

Frustration clouded Jess's pretty face. "Do we really need to talk about this right now?"

"Jess, come on. Be fair. You have to give me some time. It's my turn now and we need to talk," Rob said. "You're breaking the rules, and we have to talk about it if we're going to keep playing this game."

Jess looked exasperated. "Rules? What rules? You want me to go out with Tina's friends, and have sex with them, and that's exactly what I'm doing. I'm sorry it's not going exactly like you imagined, but you're just going to have to deal with it!" She angrily walked away.

"Jess, wait," Rob said, grabbing her arm. "Come on, we have to talk about this."

"No, we don't!" she snapped, pulling her arm away. "This is so unfair! I do exactly what you want, and then you pull this crap on me!"

"I just want you to keep it physical—just sex – that's all I'm saying."

"Well, I'm sorry!" she said angrily, starting to cry. "That's not so easy for me! You should have thought of that before we started this!" Tears were falling down Jess's cheeks.

Rob didn't understand why she was so upset. "Why are you crying?" he asked.

Jess didn't answer. She crossed her arms tightly around herself, tears flowing down her face. After so many years of marriage, Rob knew what she wanted, so he stepped closer and put his arms around her.

"Come on honey," he urged in a soft, gentle voice. "Tell me why you're so upset."

Jess hesitated for a few more moments, and then sank into his shoulder, crying. "We had an argument last night," she said sobbing.

"Who? You and Tina?"

"Noooooo," she sobbed. "Me and Darius."

———◉———

LATER THAT DAY, ROB sat in his den while Jess took a nap in their bedroom. Still tired and emotionally spent, she had fallen asleep, her cheeks still wet. "Am I being unfair?" he wondered as he looked out the window. He had cajoled her into this lifestyle. He knew many girls aren't able to have a physical relationship with a man without developing feelings. It had been entirely predictable that, if they played this game, Jess would develop feelings for the men she slept with, especially if she focused on one man, like she had with Darius.

Rob had known this when they started, and in fact that aspect of the game was often a big part of his fantasy. Last night, when he saw Jess without her wedding ring, it had hurt, but also thrilled him. The idea that Jess had developed feelings for Darius excited him. It hurt, and he knew it was dangerous, but it delighted him too, and aroused him.

He walked into their bedroom. He could tell she was awake, although she was snuggled against a pillow, her back to him. He sat on the bed and softly rubbed her back. He said, "I'm sorry for what I said earlier. You're right, I'm not being fair. I know you love me, so what I said was wrong."

Jess turned around so she faced Rob. She had stopped crying, but she still looked sad. She gripped his hand. "I do love you," she assured him.

Rob smiled reassuringly, and said, "I know you're upset about your fight last night with Darius. Why don't you go see him, and make up?"

Jess looked surprised. "I'm not sure ..." she said cautiously. "I mean, we planned to spend the day together."

Rob again smiled reassuringly. "It's all right, really. I have more work to do on that project. I know this is really bothering you, and I want you to be happy."

Jess looked amazed. "You're the most wonderful husband in the world," she said, and kissed him.

Later that evening, Rob sat alone eating dinner. An hour earlier, Jess had texted him, saying she and Darius had made up. He didn't expect her back for hours. Luckily, the kids were with Jess's parents for the weekend. But, still, that meant spending another night alone.

He tried to work but couldn't concentrate. He thought about what Jess was doing with Darius. Or, probably more accurate, what Darius was doing to her. To her body.

Jess had looked amazing when she left. She had worn a tight top with a scooped neckline, the one she loved because it made her breasts look bigger than they really were. She also wore the tiny mini-skirt he had given her for their anniversary 2 years ago. It was so short – she always said it was "obscenely short" because it was hard for her to sit without flashing her panties—she rarely wore it. To top off her outfit she wore her highest heels. She had definitely dressed to impress, and he was sure it wasn't hard for her to make up with Darius after he saw how good she looked.

Rob watched TV and tried to read. It was late, but he wasn't tired. He masturbated twice thinking about his wife with another man, the pangs of jealousy and doubt intensifying his pleasure, and then depressing him after cumming.

Around 1am he had a thought. He wondered if she had thrown the t-shirt from the contest into her closet. He went into their bedroom, and then into her walk-in closet.

There it was. Picking it up, he couldn't believe how tiny it was. The tag said it was an extra-extra small. No wonder it had looked like it was painted on her. He brought it up to his nose, and smelled cum. He remembered how Darius had cum so much it had dribbled out of her mouth. All of that excess spunk must have ended up on the t-shirt.

Glancing around her closet, Rob saw a small package on the floor. It was a package of thigh high stockings from Victoria's Secret! That shocked him, because Jess always wore pantyhose or, lately, gone bare legged with skirts and dresses (to give Darius – as Tina would say – easier access to her fun parts). Despite all his efforts over the years, he had never been able to convince Jess to wear real stockings. Once every few years she might wear stockings on their anniversary or his birthday, but that was it. She always said they were too impractical, and she felt exposed with real stockings or thigh highs ending at her mid-thigh.

The package was torn open, and empty. He opened the drawer where she kept her lingerie. As expected, he saw little bags of pantyhose. But he also saw a Victoria's Secrets bag. The receipt was still in the bag. It was two months old, and it showed she had bought a dozen thigh high stockings (mostly nude and black, but a couple bridal white), as well as garter belts. There were only two unopened packages of stockings left.

Clearly, over the last two months, Jess had been wearing stockings and garter belts for Darius. That hurt, just as much as seeing her without her wedding ring. Rob was a leg man, and Jess knew it. He worshipped her long legs, and for years he had begged her to wear thigh highs and garter belts. She never had, always saying how impractical they were. But she wore them for Darius, and had been for some time. He hadn't noticed, because they had been going to Darius place instead of Tina's for the past two months. Tess hadn't even been considerate enough to wear the stockings when she came home, so he could enjoy them when he reclaimed her.

Rob opened the drawer more and found a few worn stockings. Most were laddered, almost all around the knees, but other places too. Rob remembered how rough Darius had been last night when he had fucked Jess's face. If he did that all the time, that would explain the laddering around her knees. The thought made his cock throb in his pants.

Rob took one of the used thigh highs in his hand. It was so soft and silky. He felt along the lace top, and poked his finger in the laddering, imagining how Jess must look in the stockings. For not the first time he considered how much power a beautiful woman could have over men, especially a pretty blonde with great legs like Jess. A girl with great legs could distract an entire room of men just by wearing a short skirt. She could cause an accident in the street by innocently adjusting her stockings on the sidewalk. She could make men pant and grow uncomfortable in their pants by crossing her legs and "accidentally" showing a hint of her lacy stocking tops.

"What are you doing?" Rob heard a voice behind him say, startling him. He turned around, and saw his wife.

A knowing smile spread on Jess's face when she saw what Rob was holding. "Have you been a bad boy, playing with my underwear?" she said, clearly drunk. She wriggled her finger at him. "Come here, you naughty boy."

"No, bring that too," she added when he was about to drop the stocking back in the drawer. She pushed him on the bed and straddled his chest.

"You're drunk," Rob said.

"Guilty," Jess said with a laugh. "And you've been a bad boy." She took the stocking from him. "I see you found my stash." She seductively rolled the stocking up her arm. "Darius is just like you. He loves it when I wear stockings."

Tess studied her hand, the stocking acting like a sheer glove. "I never realized how much an aphrodisiac they were for men. I mean, I know you love them. But the first time I wore them for Darius, he practically raped me."

"Why did you start wearing them?" Rob asked. He was steel in his pants and breathing hard.

"Darius asked me to," she said simply. She spread her fingers, emphasizing the laddering in the nylon. She poked her finger through one of the rips. "They're so fragile, and Darius can get rough. Usually they don't last a single evening. So I don't have many left – but I guess you saw that. I'll need to get more soon."

She ran her stocking-clad hand across Rob's cheek. It was her left hand. He saw that, once again, she was ringless. But Rob wasn't going to mentioned that now.

Jess said, "I saved some of the stockings – the ones without too many runs – to wear when I go out with you. Would you like that?" She reached back and felt Rob's crotch, then giggled. "I see you would."

"Robbie, would you like to see the garters I wore for Darius tonight?" she teased.

Rob nodded excitedly. His throat was so dry he didn't trust himself to speak.

On her knees, straddling Rob's chest, Jess pulled up her tiny mini-skirt. He stopped breathing as the lacy stocking tops came into view. Then, as she inched up her skirt, he saw the smooth firm skin of her thighs, and the straps of her garter belt. The straps were black, matching her stockings, and had lace edging.

"When Darius fucks me, he likes to put his hand in my stockings. Like this." Jess took her husband's hand. "First he does this," she said, running his fingers along the garter strap, first along the lacy edging, and then the inner side of the strap pressed against her thigh.

"Then he does this," and Jess edged Rob's hand inside her stocking. "Darius says he likes how it feels, feeling the stocking against the back of his hand as he touches my thigh. Do you like that too, Robbie?"

"Yeah," Rob groaned. His heart was pounding. He felt like he was going to explode.

She giggled. "I thought you would." She ran her fingertip over the nylon covering his hand. The laddering was getting worse from the stress caused by Rob's hand.

"Now you see how my stockings get ruined," Jess said. "But the runs around my knees are really bad. Can you guess why?"

Yes, Rob could guess why. He had just been thinking about it earlier that evening. But hearing her confirm it was incredibly exciting.

Jess seemed to read his thoughts, and seductively smiled. She reached back and stroked him through his pants. "Tina told me she sent you that video. Darius using me in the alley after the wet t-shirt contest. You saw how rough he was with me. Did you like seeing that?"

"Yeeesssssss!" Rob growled.

"He's always like that, so rough with me," Tess said with a pretend pout. "I like it, but it ruins my stockings." She pointed to her knees. "Look."

Rob looked down and saw the laddering around her knees. Jess had him so worked up, he was close to cumming in his pants.

Jess knew it and rubbed him harder. "He always cums so much, I can't swallow it all. He tastes different from you, but I like it. In his car, a few minutes ago, I went down on him. It was so exciting. One of our neighbors could have walked by and seen me. I think it excited Darius too, because he came even more than usual. But I managed to swallow most of it. I can still taste him in my mouth."

Suddenly, Jess leaned over and kissed her husband, thrusting her tongue into his mouth. Rob tasted something bitter that he knew was the remnants of Darius's semen in her mouth. The nastiness made him lightheaded.

Rob urgently rolled Jess onto her back. He tore off his pants and boxers.

He pushed Jess's skirt up farther, so it was up around her waist. Now he was able to see all of her long, shapely legs in the real stockings and the garter belt. He also saw she wasn't wearing panties.

Rob had never been so excited in his life. He thrusted into Jess's pussy. He pumped into his wife once, twice, a third time, and then he was cumming. He shot his spunk into his wife, although his sperm (unlike Darius's) could no longer get a girl pregnant. Ever since his vasectomy, he had been shooting blanks into Jess.

After cumming, Rob kissed Jess, and she cradled his head in her arms. "I love you, I love you," he said over an over again. "You're so perfect."

"I'm so lucky to have you as my husband," Jess said as she lazily played with Rob's hair.

Rob got up on his elbow and looked into Jess's pretty face. "What was the fight about anyway?" he asked. "Between you and Darius?"

"I don't know actually," Jess said with a helpless laugh. "You know, he's young, and full of hormones. And I'm older. Sometimes, you know, I guess we get out of sync."

"Out of sync ...," Rob repeated, processing what she just said. Jess was in a relationship with another man.

His *wife* was in a relationship with another man.

Not just sex. A *relationship*. It was like they were boyfriend and girlfriend.

And sometimes boyfriends and girlfriends got out of sync. And had arguments.

"Hey, are you okay?" Jess asked as she looked up into her husband's face. "Are you upset I don't wear my rings when I'm with Darius?"

"Ooops, I forgot," Jess said. She reached for her purse and retrieve her wedding and engagement rings from the zippered pouch. She put them back on the ring finger of her left hand.

Robb rolled off of his wife. His softening cock had already slipped out of her pussy. He lay on his side looking at her.

Rob put his hand on the lacy top of Jess's stocking. He said, "I'm more upset you're wearing these for him and not me." He kept his tone light as he didn't want Jess to think he was attacking her, but it did hurt him.

"I'm sorry about that," Jess said, affectionately brushing her hand against her husband's cheek. "I guess since I'm so much older – I mean, Rob, I'm 13 years older than him – I guess I feel like I need to do things to keep him interested in me."

"Yeah, I guess I understand that," Rob said. What Jess said made sense. But he wished she felt that way about him. He wished she felt she had to wear sexy lingerie to keep *him* interested in her. But why should she, though? For their entire relationship, he had been the one chasing her. He still couldn't believe she had picked him to marry. Their friends

– like Tina – felt the same way. They all liked Rob – he was a nice guy – but Jess was way better in the looks department than her husband.

"Are you okay with everything, Robbie? I mean, what we're doing? My relationship with Darius?"

"You're not going to leave me for him, are you?" Rob asked. He said it jokingly, but there was vulnerability in his voice. He was worried about this.

"No, I'm not going to leave you for him," Jess said with a playful slap across Rob's chest. "We have our life together, our kids, I love you. No Robbie, that will never happen. And anyways, I *am* a lot older than Darius. I'm just his latest MILF-toy, he'll move on to another one eventually."

"Okay, well, that's good," Rob said with a laugh. Jess's words didn't exactly reassure him.

Jess could tell her husband was still worried. Looking apologetic, she said, "I'm sorry, it's just complicated –."

Rob completed her sentence, saying, "It's complicated when you add a third person."

"Yeah," Jess said with a laugh, but the laugh was without any humor.

The married couple looked at each other for a long moment. Then Jess asked, "Are we going to be okay, Robbie?"

Rob looked down his wife's body. Her skirt was still up around her waist, revealing her garter belt, thigh high stockings and 4-inch stiletto high heels. He had never seen her looking so good.

So sexy.

The fact she had just been with another man made her even sexier.

He felt himself getting hard again.

"Yeah, we'll be okay," Rob said as he rolled on top of his wife. They kissed and fondled until he was completely hard again. Then Rob penetrated Jess's pussy with his hard cock, and he reclaimed his wife again.

They made love again.

If You Like Happy Endings, Then Stop Reading Here!

Otherwise, Read The Next Chapter, Husband's Fantasy Backfires Book 2

YOU'VE BEEN WARNED!!!

Don't miss out!

Visit the website below and you can sign up to receive emails whenever Pete Andrews publishes a new book. There's no charge and no obligation.

https://books2read.com/r/B-A-KWSAB-EUGCF

BOOKS 2 READ

Connecting independent readers to independent writers.

Also by Pete Andrews

Be Careful What You Wish For
Be Careful What You Wish For Book 1
A Cuckold Fiancée and a Cuckquean Wife - Be Careful What You Wish For Book 2
My Girl Is Another Man's Date - Be Careful What You Wish For Book 3
My Fiancee Skin-To-Skin With Another Man - Be Careful What You Wish For Book 4
Groom Watches New Bride With Another Man - Be Careful What You Wish For Book 5
Bride With Rival On Honeymoon - Be Careful What You Wish For Book 6

Faithful Wife's Fall From Grace
Faithful Wife's Fall From Grace Book 1
Faithful Wife's Fall From Grace Book 2
Faithful Wife's Fall From Grace Book 3
Faithful Wife's Fall From Grace Book 4
Faithful Wife's Fall From Grace Book 5
Faithful Wife's Fall From Grace Book 6
Faithful Wife's Fall From Grace Book 7
Faithful Wife's Fall From Grace Book 8

Flash Of Stocking Collection
Wife Watching Game And Other Stories: Flash of Stocking
Collection 1
Wife Dates Another Man and Other Stories: Flash of Stocking
Collection 2
Losing My Wife To Another Man - Three Interracial Cuckold
Novellas: Flash of Stocking Collection 3

Girls Who Belong To Other Men
Girls Who Belong To Other Men Book 1
Girls Who Belong To Other Men Book 2

Husband's Fantasy Backfires
Husband's Fantasy Backfires - Book 1

Opening Pandora's Box
Opening Pandora's Box 1 - Jessie Plays For Her Husband
Opening Pandora's Box 2 - Ollie Watches His Wife With Another
Man
Opening Pandora's Box 3 - Jessie Grows Closer To Roman
Opening Pandora's Box 4 - Jessie Loses Herself In Roman
Opening Pandora's Box 5 - How Can You Do This To Me?

Tiny Dancer: A Modern Romance

Tiny Dancer: A Young Cuckold Romance Book 1
Tiny Dancer: A Modern Romance Book 2
Tiny Dancer: A Young Cuckold Romance Book 3

Standalone
Playing At Work Is Dangerous: A Reluctant Wife Story